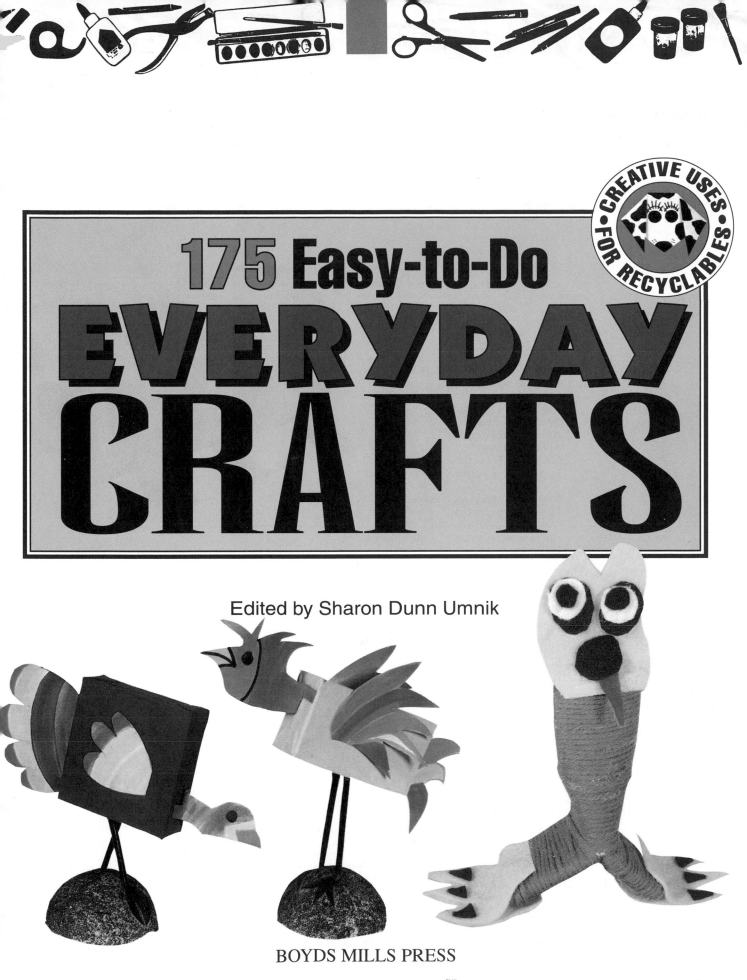

175 Easy-to-Do
EVERYDAY CRAFTS

CREATIVE USES · FOR RECYCLABLES

Edited by Sharon Dunn Umnik

BOYDS MILLS PRESS

Inside this book...
you'll find a fabulous assortment of crafts made from
recyclable items and inexpensive things found in
or around your house. Have pencils, crayons,
scissors, tape, paintbrushes, and other supplies for craft
making close by. – *the Editor*

Copyright © 1995 by Boyds Mills Press
All rights reserved

Published by Bell Books
Boyds Mills Press, Inc.
A Highlights Company
815 Church Street
Honesdale, Pennsylvania 18431
Printed in the United States of America

Publisher Cataloging-in-Publication Data
Main entry under title :
    175 easy-to-do everyday crafts : creative uses for recyclables /
edited by Sharon Dunn Umnik.—1st ed.
[64]p. : col. ill. ; cm.
Summary : Includes step-by-step directions to make simple crafts from
household items.
ISBN 1-56397-441-X
1. Handicraft—Juvenile literature. [1. Handicraft.] I. Umnik, Sharon Dunn.
II. Title.
745.5—dc20   1995   CIP
Library of Congress Catalog Card Number: 94-72626

First edition, 1995
Book designed by Charlie Cary
The text of this book is set in 11-point New Century Schoolbook.
Distributed by St. Martin's Press

10 9 8 7 6 5 4 3

Craft Contributors: Helen Afana, Laura Arlon, Jennifer Arnold, Denwood Barksdale, Kathy Bayly, Laura G.
Beer, Barbara Bell, Peg Biegler, Linda Bloomgren, Peggy Boozer, Doris Boutin, Phil A. Bowie, Eunice Bremer,
Judy Chiss, Sandra E. Csippan, Peggy Welton De Shan, Ruth Dougherty, Linda Douglas, Marianne J. Dyson,
Susan P. Easter, Laurie Edwards, Kathy Everett, Clara Flammang, JoAnn Fluegeman, Carole Forman,
Nancy H. Giles, Sid Gilmer, Sandra Godfrey, Monica M. Graham, Mavis Grant, Mary Alma Harper, Edna
Harrington, Nan Hathaway, Patricia O. Hester, Barbara Hill, Olive Howie, Helen Jeffries, Ruth Ann Johnson,
Tama Kain, Garnett C. Kooker, Kathy Kranch, Virginia L. Kroll, K.S. Kubona, Twilla Lamm, Lila LeBaron,
Janet Rose Lehmberg, Ann Lewandowski, Lee Lindeman, Marion Bonsteel Lyke, Lory MacRae, Agnes Maddy,
Linda K. Marchi, H. Marcin, JoAnn Markway, Carol McCall, Mary Minerman, Clare Mishica, June Rose
Mobly, Patricia Moseser, Bridget Pakenham Murphy, Mary Ellen Norlen, Helen M. Pedersen, Beatrice
Bachrach Perri, James W. Perrin Jr., Judy Peterson, Louise Poe, Jane K. Priewe, Necia Sneed Ramsey, Kathy
Ross, S.R. Shaphren, Mary Shea, Dorothea V. Shull, Andrew J. Smith, Barbara Smith, Romy Squeri, Darcy
Mason Swope, Mary S. Toth, Sharon Dunn Umnik, Joy Warrell, Patricia Wilson, D.A. Woodliff, Norma
Bennett Woolf, Jabeen Y. Yusufali, Peg Ziegler, and Patsy Zimmerman.

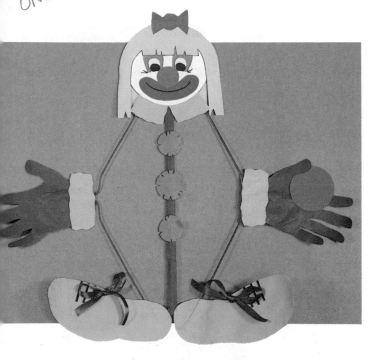

HANGER PEOPLE
(two wire clothes hangers, construction paper, ribbon)

1. Tape together the bottoms of two wire clothes hangers.

2. Cut two large identical construction paper circles for the head. Glue the circles together with one end of the hanger in between them. Glue on cut-paper features and hair.

3. On paper, trace around each of your hands and feet twice. Cut them out.

4. Place one of the cutout left hands on top of the hook of one hanger and one of the right hands underneath. Glue the hands together. Do the same to the other hook. Glue the feet on the other end of the hanger, opposite the head.

5. Decorate the shoes with ribbon.

BUTTON BAUBLE PINS
(lightweight cardboard, buttons, safety pin, felt)

1. Cut small shapes from lightweight cardboard. Glue buttons on the cardboard shapes and let them dry.

2. Hold a safety pin by the side that opens, and glue the other side to the back of the cardboard. Do this with each button pin.

3. Cut a small narrow strip of felt for each button pin. Glue the strip to the cardboard and across the back of each safety pin. When dry, wear the pin or give as a gift.

WATERMELON CHECKERBOARD
(heavy corrugated cardboard, poster paint, black permanent marker, twelve watermelon seeds, twelve squash seeds)

1. Cut a circle about 14 inches wide from heavy corrugated cardboard. Paint the outer inch of the circle with green poster paint. Paint the inside of the circle red. Paint a thin white line where the two colors meet.

2. With a pencil, draw an 8-inch square in the red area. Mark off every inch on each side of the square. Connect the marks on opposite sides of the square, dividing it into sixty-four small squares.

3. With a permanent black marker, outline the large square. Color in every other small square to form a checkerboard. Draw on watermelon seeds.

4. Use twelve black seeds from a watermelon and twelve white seeds from a squash as your game's playing pieces.

AUTOGRAPH POOCH
(brown paper bag, crayons or markers)

1. Cut a large brown paper bag into a rectangle 18 inches long and 6 inches wide. On the long edges of the paper, make pencil marks 6 inches in from each end.

2. Fold the ends of the paper toward the center at these marks. Fold the ends back to meet those folds.

3. Open up the paper. Draw a dog across the whole piece of paper, with its head on the far right panel and its tail end on the far left.

4. Draw a collar or bandanna on the dog, and put your name on it.

5. Have your friends sign your Autograph Pooch at the end of the school year. Or give a Pooch, signed by your whole class, to your teacher.

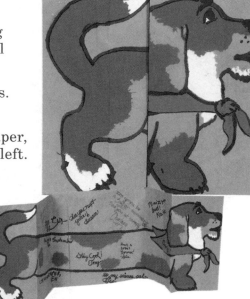

SPONGE PAINTING
(cellulose sponge, poster paint, poster board)

1. Cut several shapes from a cellulose sponge (the kind that has irregular holes).

2. Dip the sponge shapes in paint, and blot them on a piece of scrap paper to remove any extra paint.

3. Paint a picture by dabbing the sponge shapes onto a piece of poster board.

YARN AND BEAD BANGLE
(metal first-aid tape container, yarn, twelve beads)

1. Tie one end of a strand of yarn, several yards long, around the cover of a metal first-aid tape container. Tape the knot to the inside.

2. Roll the strand of yarn into a small ball to make it easy to handle. Tightly wrap the yarn around the entire cover, keeping the strands close together.

3. Cut the yarn, leaving a 6-inch tail. Loop the tail under a few of the strands on the inside of the cover, knot it, and trim.

4. Tie one end of a 20-inch strand of yarn to the inside of the cover. String twelve or more beads on it.

5. Wrap the yarn and beads around the cover to form a design on the bracelet. On the inside, loop the tail under a few strands, knot it, and trim the end.

PAPIER-MÂCHÉ PETS
(newspaper, flour and water, aluminum foil, poster paint, string)

1. Cover your work area with lots of newspaper. Mix 1 cup of flour with 1 cup of water to make a paste.

2. Wad up pieces of newspaper to form a core for the animal you want to make. Tear small strips of newspaper and dip them into the paste. Place the strips on the core, forming the animal's body.

3. Add more newspaper wads for legs and the head. Mold paste-covered strips of paper around them with your hands.

4. Place the papier-mâché pets on aluminum foil and let them dry overnight, or until they are hard. Then paint the pets, adding details with string.

"BOOK" BOOKENDS
(two corrugated-cardboard packing boxes, small stones, plastic food-storage bags, construction paper, markers)

1. Fill two corrugated-cardboard packing boxes with unpopped popcorn, small stones, or sand in plastic bags. Tape the lids shut.

2. Decorate the boxes with strips of construction paper and markers, making them look like books lined up on a shelf.

3. Write your favorite book titles along the book "bindings."

4. Use the "book" bookends to hold your books upright on a shelf.

SOAP BASKET
(plastic food container, fabric, ribbon)

1. Place an empty round plastic food container in the center of a piece of fabric. With a ruler, measure the height of the container. Add 1 to 1 1/2 inches to that measurement.

2. With the ruler, measure the fabric starting from the bottom of the container until you reach the total measurement. Make small marks with a pencil, going all the way around the container. You should see a circle forming. Remove the container and cut out the circle.

3. Squeeze glue along the inside rim of the container. Place the container in the center of the fabric and pull the fabric up over the rim and into the glue. Work the fabric evenly around the rim and let dry. Tie a ribbon around the outside. Place soaps in the basket.

THE BANK BUILDING

(cocoa container with round metal lid, construction paper)

1. Wash and dry an empty cocoa container.

2. Cover the sides of the container with glue and a piece of construction paper. Turn the container so the round metal lid is on the bottom. Glue pieces of paper to the top to make it look like a roof.

3. Using cut paper, decorate the rest of the container to look like a bank building.

4. On the back of the bank, have an adult help you cut a slit just under the roof, large enough to slip money through.

5. After you have filled the bank building with coins and bills, pop open the round metal lid to remove the money and deposit it into a real bank.

MINIATURE BOOK BOOKMARK

(felt, paper, newspaper)

1. Cut a small rectangle of felt and fold it in half, making a book cover. Cut three pieces of paper the same size as the rectangle.

2. Fold the pieces of paper in half, place them in the book, and staple them from the outside in the center along the fold.

3. Cut two long felt strips and glue them inside the back of the book. Trim the ends by cutting an upside-down V shape into them.

4. Cut out a title from an old newspaper and glue it to the front of the book, or write one with a pen on a piece of paper.

FARMHAND PUPPETS

(felt, old cotton glove, thread)

1. Cut five felt circles just large enough to cover your fingertips.

2. Place an old cotton glove palm-side up. Glue a felt circle to each fingertip to make an animal head.

3. Cut and glue felt pieces on the circles to make facial features for each animal. Add pieces of thread for whiskers. Let dry.

4. Place your hand inside the glove, and make up your own puppet play.

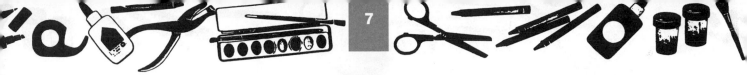

STARLIGHT MOBILE
(lightweight cardboard, aluminum foil, tinsel, thread)

1. Cut a crescent moon and three star shapes from lightweight cardboard. Trace around each shape twice onto aluminum foil and cut out the shapes.

2. Glue the foil crescents to each side of the cardboard moon.

3. Glue tinsel to each of the cardboard stars. Glue the foil stars to each side of the cardboard stars.

4. Tape a dark-colored thread from each star to the moon. Glue a long piece of thread along the inside curve of the moon.

5. When the glue dries, hang the mobile in a window.

DANCIN' HUMPTY DUMPTY
(poster board, construction paper, chenille sticks, string, yarn)

1. Cut two large identically sized egg shapes from poster board.

2. For Humpty Dumpty's front, decorate one egg shape with facial features cut from construction paper and chenille sticks. Use the other egg shape for his back and decorate.

3. Place chenille-stick arms and legs between the two egg shapes. Use tape and glue to attach the shapes together.

4. Cut four hand shapes and four shoe shapes from paper. Glue two hands to the end of each arm, and glue two shoe shapes to the end of each leg.

5. Punch a hole in the top of the egg and tie a string through it. Add a large yarn pompon for hair. Bounce the string to see Humpty Dumpty dance.

RING TOSS
(corrugated cardboard, masking tape, poster paint, pushpins,
plastic-ring beverage holder)

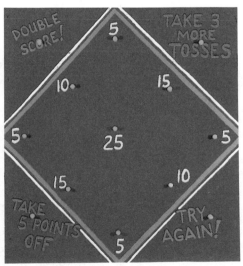

1. Glue two 18-by-20-inch pieces of corrugated cardboard back to back to make a game board. Cover the edges with masking tape.

2. Paint the game board and let it dry. Then paint numbers and scoring directions on the board, as shown.

3. Put glue on the bottom of a pushpin. Push the pin into the board at one of the painted numbers. Repeat with more pushpins—one for each of the numbers. (If the pins come through the back of the game board, cover them with cotton and masking tape.)

4. Cut plastic rings from a six-pack beverage holder. To play the game, toss the rings at the game board and add up your score.

CEREAL BOX SCRAPBOOK
(cereal box, gift wrap, brown paper bags, shoelace)

1. Cut out the front, bottom, and back from a cereal box in one piece. Glue on gift wrap to cover it.

2. To make pages, cut pieces the same size as the book cover from brown paper bags.

3. Punch two holes in the front and back covers, then punch holes in the pages, making sure all holes line up.

4. Place the pages between the covers. Pull a shoelace through the holes in the back cover, through the pages, and to the front cover. Tie the shoelace into a bow.

RIBBON PICTURE HOLDER
(white poster board, old greeting cards, ribbon)

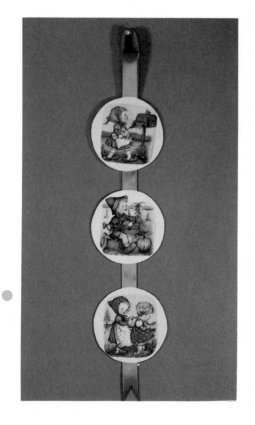

1. Cut three circles from white poster board. Cut pictures from old greeting cards and glue them on top of the circles.

2. Cut a long piece of ribbon. Make a loop in the ribbon at one end and staple it. Cut a small piece of ribbon. Place it through the first loop and staple the ends together for a hanger.

3. Glue the three circles with pictures to the long piece of ribbon. Let dry and then hang up.

PLASTIC-BOX FISH TANK
(greeting card box with clear acetate top, construction paper, yarn)

1. Cut and glue construction paper inside a greeting card box that has a clear acetate top.

2. Cut out fish and seaweed from paper. Glue them inside the box.

3. Place the clear acetate top on the box. Cut a piece of yarn and glue or tape it to the back of the box for a hanger.

TWINE PLANTER
(cardboard food container, clear plastic from a greeting card box, white cotton cord, poster paint)

1. Wash and dry a cardboard food container like one in which peanuts are packaged.

2. Start at the bottom of the container and spread a little glue around the outside. Press the end of a long piece of white cotton cord into the glue, and wind the cord around the container until it is covered.

3. To make a stencil, cut a small plastic square from a greeting card box. Draw a flower in the middle. Start in the middle of the flower and cut it out, leaving a border of plastic around it. Do the same for a stem and leaves.

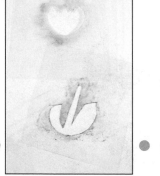

4. Dip a dry brush in just a little poster paint. Wipe the brush on a towel to get rid of excess paint.

5. Hold the stencil for the stem and leaves near the base of the container. Rub the dry brush over the cutout stem and leaves. The paint will fill the cutout area. Do the same for the flower.

FOOT PICTURES
(construction paper, buttons, chenille sticks, yarn, fabric)

1. Trace around your shoe on a sheet of light-colored construction paper.

2. Create a character by decorating the shoe outline with buttons, chenille sticks, yarn, fabric, and markers.

HANDY-DANDY HANGER
(wire clothes hanger, lightweight cardboard, fabric, spring-type clothespins, lace or ribbon)

1. Lay a wire clothes hanger on a piece of cardboard and trace around the outside with a pencil. Do this again and cut out the two pieces.

2. Place the hanger between the two cardboard pieces and tape them tightly together. Cover with glue and fabric.

3. Glue spring-type clothespins to the fabric. Decorate with lace or ribbon.

4. Hang scarves, ribbons, or hair clips from the clothespins.

WALLPAPER PLACE MATS
(wallpaper, poster board, yarn)

1. Cut a piece of wallpaper to measure 9 inches by 13 inches. Cut a piece of poster board the same size.

2. If you use prepasted wallpaper, wet the back with a little warm water. If you use a piece of plain wallpaper, spread glue on the back. Press the paper onto the poster board.

3. Make the border by punching holes around the edges with a paper punch. Weave a piece of yarn in and out of the holes.

4. Join the ends together and tie a bow.

CEREAL-BOX CAR
(cereal box, felt or construction paper, cardboard)

1. Tape the flaps of a cereal box closed. Follow the diagrams to create a car shape by cutting and folding.

2. Cover the car with felt or paper. Cut tires and a steering wheel from cardboard. Add felt or paper and glue them to the car.

3. Finish the car with a license plate, lights, and door handles. Add a couple of passengers.

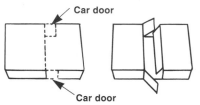

PAPER-PLATE MONKEY
(two paper plates, construction paper)

1. Place two paper plates on top of each other, right-side up. Staple them together halfway around the edges. Fold each unstapled plate-half over the stapled section.

2. Place your fingers inside the pocket created. Note where your thumb falls on the back, and tape on a paper loop for your thumb to slide into.

3. Decorate the plate with paper and markers to make the monkey.

PLASTIC CIRCLE BRACELET
(large plastic lid, yarn, tape)

1. Draw 1-inch circles on a large plastic lid. Cut them out with scissors.

2. With a paper punch, punch two holes, one opposite the other, in each plastic circle.

3. Cut an 18-inch piece of yarn. Make a point with a small piece of tape on one end of the yarn, like a needle.

4. Weave the yarn through the circles. When finished, cut the tape off and tie the ends of the yarn into a bow.

SHOPPER'S HELPERS
(envelopes, old magazines)

1. Cut out pictures of food or other household items from old magazines. Glue the pictures on one end of an envelope.

2. Below the pictures, make lines for items on a shopping list. Make a special column to check if there's a coupon.

3. Place any coupons inside the envelope. Take the envelope with you when you shop for groceries.

HORSESHOE PAPERWEIGHT
(corrugated cardboard, poster paint, small stones)

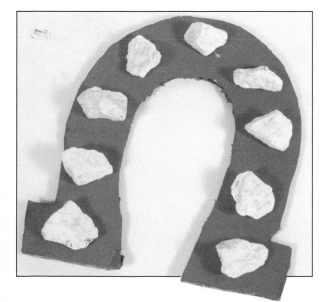

1. Cut a horseshoe shape from a piece of corrugated cardboard. Paint it a bright color.

2. Select an assortment of small stones that are all about the same size and thickness. Wash them and let dry.

3. Paint the stones a contrasting color to the horseshoe.

4. When the paint is dry, glue the stones around the horseshoe.

STRAW-BACKED PORCUPINE

(one 2- and one 3-inch plastic-foam ball, table knife, ice-cream stick, poster paint, sponge, felt, plastic drinking straws)

1. Cut a 3-inch plastic-foam ball in half with a table knife. Use one half for the body and save the other half for another craft.

2. Break an ice-cream stick in half. Put glue on one end of the stick, and push it into the body for the neck. Put glue on the other end of the stick, and push a 2-inch plastic-foam ball onto it for the head. Cover the body with poster paint, using a small piece of sponge, and let dry.

3. Place the body on a piece of felt, trace around it, and add four feet and a tail. Cut out the felt shape and glue it to the bottom of the body. Cut out facial features from felt, and glue in place. Make a small slit above each eye and push in pieces of felt for the ears.

4. Using a pencil, poke holes in the body, head, and tail. Put glue in each hole, and insert small pieces of plastic drinking straws for quills.

MILK CAP PENDANT

(plastic milk cap, ribbon)

1. Cut a photo to fit inside a plastic milk cap. Glue the photo inside the cap.

2. Cut a ribbon long enough to go around your neck and tie it together at the ends.

3. Glue the back of the milk cap to the ribbon.

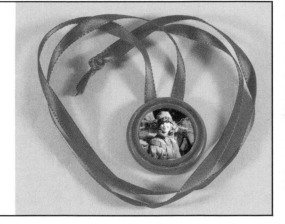

AIRPLANE

(two paper towel tubes, one bathroom tissue tube, poster paint, three ice-cream sticks)

1. Measure 3 inches from one end of a paper towel tube and draw a line. Measure 2 inches from this point, draw another line, and cut the small 2-inch section from half of the tube. Insert another paper towel tube crosswise for the wing section, attaching the two tubes with glue.

2. For the tail, cut a slit on each side of the body at the other end of the tube. Glue a small bathroom tissue tube between the slits.

3. Paint three ice-cream sticks. Glue two together to form an X. Glue them to the front of the airplane for the propeller.

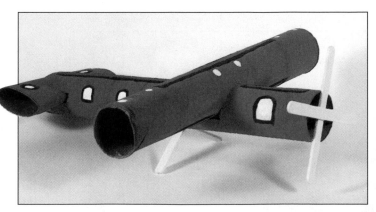

4. Break one ice-cream stick in half. Poke a hole through the bottom of the plane, and glue the sticks in place for the landing gear. Paint on windows and other details.

CLEVER GIFT BAGS
(brown paper bag, construction paper)

1. From construction paper, draw and cut out animal features.

2. Glue the features to one side of a paper bag for the front of the animal.

3. Cut out features for the back of the animal to decorate the back of the bag.

4. Create cats, dogs, and other animals.

● ● ● ● ● ● ● ● ● ● ● ● ● ● ● ●

TOUCH-ME NUMBER POSTER
(ten of some object such as buttons, nine of another object, and so on down to one object, cardboard)

1. Collect interesting small objects that are alike. You'll need ten of some object, nine of another, and so on. Plan ahead so you have room for everything.

2. Draw ten evenly spaced lines across a piece of cardboard, leaving space at the top for a title.

3. Add the title using markers or paper.

4. Draw the number 1 on the first line and glue on one object (maybe a balloon). On the second line, draw the number 2 and glue on two objects that are alike. Continue writing numbers and adding objects until you complete the number 10.

FELT APPLE PINCUSHION
(felt, needle and thread, cotton balls)

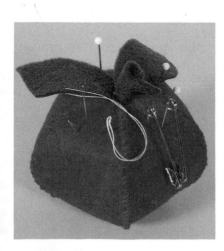

1. Cut five felt pieces using the pattern shown. Sew them together with seams facing out to form the apple shape.

2. Stuff the apple with cotton balls before sewing the last seam closed.

3. Cut a strip of felt and roll it into a stem. Stitch it to the apple. Cut felt leaves and stitch those to the apple. Place sewing pins in the apple.

Trace or copy this pattern for your felt pieces.

DECOUPAGE PENCIL HOLDER
(frozen-juice container, green construction paper, white glue and water, bowl,
old flower catalogs, clear nail polish)

1. Cover the outside of a frozen-juice container with green construction paper. Cut pictures of different kinds of flowers from an old flower catalog.

2. Mix white glue and a little water together in a bowl. Brush the glue mixture on the backs of the flower cutouts and place them around the container.

3. When the container is covered with flowers, brush a little of the glue mixture over the entire outside of the container and let dry.

4. Give the flowers a shiny finish with coats of clear nail polish.

STICK FRAME
(four ice-cream sticks, yarn)

1. Glue four ice-cream sticks together to form a square frame.

2. Attach a picture or photo with glue, and let dry.

3. Glue a piece of yarn to the back for a hanger.

A FUNNY STORYBOOK
(old magazines, construction paper,
white writing paper, yarn,
self-adhesive reinforcement rings)

1. Cut out ten pictures from old magazines.

2. Take five pieces of construction paper and glue one picture on each side. Leave room under each picture to glue a 4-by-6-inch piece of white writing paper.

3. Write a story from one picture to the next on the white paper.

4. Make a front and back cover for the book from construction paper. Write the title on the front with markers or crayons.

5. Holding the pages in order, punch holes on the left side. Place self-adhesive reinforcement rings over the holes, and tie pieces of yarn through the holes to keep the book together.

SPONGE HAND PUPPETS
(soft sponges, construction paper)

1. In the edge of a sponge, cut a slit large enough so your three middle fingers will fit inside.

2. From construction paper, cut out a mouth, eyes, ears, and a nose for each puppet. Glue them in place. The ears can be glued to the back side of the sponge.

3. Put your middle fingers inside and let your thumb and little finger represent the puppet's arms.

GET-WELL MESSAGE
(round oatmeal container, gift wrap, table knife, paper)

1. Measure 2 1/2 inches up from the bottom of a round oatmeal container. Cut off the top part, but save the lid for later.

2. Glue gift wrap around the sides and the lid. Draw a face on the bottom. Then, using a table knife, make a slit about 1 1/2 inches wide for a mouth.

3. Cut a long strip of plain paper, narrower than the mouth opening. Write a get-well message on the strip. Add jokes and riddles or write a story.

4. Roll the strip around a pencil and place the message inside the box. Thread the beginning of the message through the mouth. Pull the strip to read the message.

CARRYING CASE FOR GLASSES
(fabric, poster board, rickrack)

1. Cut two pieces of fabric 8 inches square. Cut a piece of poster board the same size and place it between the fabric squares. Glue all the layers together.

2. Fold in half. Glue the long side and one short side together. Leave the other short side unglued as an opening for the glasses.

3. Decorate the front by gluing on pieces of rickrack to make a design. Let dry overnight.

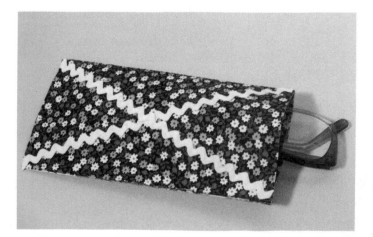

DOORKNOB HANGER
(poster board, old magazines)

1. Cut out a piece of poster board 4 inches wide and 8 inches long.

2. Measure down about an inch on the long side of the poster board and draw a circle in the middle, about 1 1/2 to 2 inches in diameter.

3. With scissors, cut a slit from the edge of the board to the middle of the circle. Cut out the circle so the hanger will fit over the doorknob.

4. Write your name with a marker and add paper cutouts from old magazines.

STRIPED CATERPILLAR
(round oatmeal container, felt, chenille stick, bathroom tissue tube, poster paint)

1. Cover a round oatmeal container with glue and strips of colored felt. For the face, glue eyes, a mouth, and a nose cut from felt onto the bottom of the container.

2. With a pencil, poke two holes (2 inches apart, 1 inch back from the face) on top of the head. Insert a chenille stick into one hole. Then reach inside the container and push the other end of the stick through the other hole. Curl the ends with a pencil.

3. Cut three 1-inch rings from the bathroom tissue tube. Cut the rings in half and paint them black. Once they dry, glue three halves to each side of the caterpillar for feet.

4. With the cover as the caterpillar's tail, you can use the caterpillar as a storage container.

DINOSAUR
(large and small toothpaste boxes,
gray construction paper)

1. Using large and small toothpaste boxes, cut sections to form the dinosaur. Use one box for the main body.

2. Cut the box sections for the neck and tail on an angle, as shown. Cut smaller box sections for the head and legs.

3. Cover each section with gray construction paper. Glue the sections together and let dry.

4. Draw eyes and a mouth with a marker.

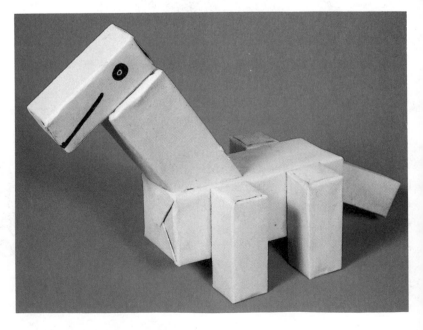

PARTY HAT
(paper, yarn)

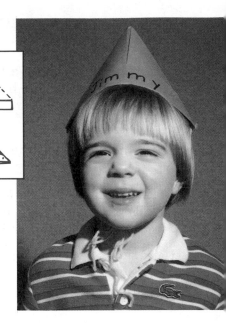

1. Fold a 9-by-12-inch sheet of paper in half. Place it in front of you with the fold at the top.

2. Fold each top corner down.

3. Take hold of the upper sheet at the bottom and fold it over the turned-down corners. Turn the hat over and do the same to the other side.

4. Turn down the little tabs that are sticking out and staple them in place.

5. Punch a hole at each side of the hat. Tie a piece of yarn in each hole to tie the hat on your head.

(You can make bigger hats by using sheets of newspaper or gift wrap, or make tiny ones for your dolls from half sheets of paper.)

ONE-SEASON BIRDHOUSE
(half-gallon milk carton, masking tape, brown shoe polish, cloth, cord)

1. Wash and dry a half-gallon milk carton. With the spout out, staple the top shut, as shown.

2. Tear off small pieces of masking tape and cover the entire milk carton. Using a soft cloth, rub brown shoe polish over the masking tape, giving it a rough, barklike look.

3. Cut an entrance hole about 4 1/2 inches above the floor. The hole should be a little less than 1 1/2 inches across.

4. Poke some small drainage holes in the floor and two ventilation holes near the top of the carton below the spout.

5. Use a paper punch to punch a hole in the top of the house. Thread a piece of cord through the hole and tie the birdhouse to a tree limb.

INITIAL PENDANT
(paper, plastic food wrap, yarn, glue)

1. Draw the outline of an initial of your name on a piece of paper. Cover the paper with plastic food wrap. Tape at the corners to hold in place.

2. Squeeze glue over the initial. Cut and press pieces of yarn onto the glue. Paint the yarn with a coat of glue.

3. Glue a loop of yarn at the top. When dry, peel the yarn letter away from the plastic. Thread a long piece of yarn through the loop.

LACED BEAR PUPPET
(large brown paper bag, yarn)

1. Cut down the seam of a large brown paper bag. Then cut the bottom out of the bag so that you have a long flat sheet of brown paper.

2. Fold the paper in half and draw a bear shape on it. Holding the paper together, cut out two bear shapes the same size.

3. Draw on features with crayons or markers. Holding the bears together, punch holes around the outside edges, leaving the bottom unpunched.

4. Lace the bears together with a piece of long yarn, weaving in and out of the holes. Tie a knot at the ends. Place your hand inside the bear to work the puppet.

TWIST-TIE PICTURE
(paper- and plastic-coated twist-ties, construction paper)

1. Collect paper- and plastic-coated twist-ties that are left over from all types of food packages. Gather a variety of colors.

2. Select a piece of construction paper for the background.

3. The twists can be left in blocks of color, separated, or cut into shapes, using scissors. Wrap the twists around a pencil to make curls.

4. Using glue, attach the twists to the paper to create a picture.

KEEPSAKE BOX
(shoe box, brown wrapping paper, old magazines)

1. Cover a shoe box and lid with brown wrapping paper. Think of a theme that you would like the keepsake box to represent. If you like horses, for example, cut out horse pictures from old magazines or an old calendar. If you like baseball, cut out baseball pictures.

2. Decorate the outside of the box with these theme pictures. Store mementoes in the box.

OCTOPUS
(cardboard egg carton, heavy yarn, paper, poster paint)

1. Glue together two cup sections from the bottom of a cardboard egg carton. Cover them with paint and let dry.

2. Glue eight heavy yarn tentacles to the bottom.

3. Cut eyes and a mouth from paper, and glue them in place.

OVER THE MOON
(poster board, paper plate, two brass fasteners)

1. Make a cow from poster board. Add features with markers.

2. Draw a face on a paper plate to make it look like the moon.

3. With a brass fastener, attach the cow to one end of a strip of poster board. Use a second brass fastener to attach the other end of the strip to the center of the plate.

4. By moving the cow around the plate, you can make the cow jump over the moon.

BOTTLE HOOPLA
(plastic food bottle, pebbles, one 1 1/2-inch plastic-foam ball, construction paper, moveable plastic eyes, push-pull detergent cap, three plastic lids)

1. Wash the plastic food bottle and scrub off the label. Put some pebbles in the bottle so it will not tip over easily.

2. For the head, firmly push and twist a 1 1/2-inch plastic-foam ball over the neck of the bottle. For the hat, push and twist a push-pull detergent cap onto the head.

3. Decorate with construction paper cutouts. Glue on moveable plastic eyes.

4. Cut the centers from three plastic lids, leaving the rims, to use as hoops. (Be sure they are the right size to "ring" the bottle figure.)

5. Score one point for each ringer.

BOX MOBILE
(three small cardboard boxes, construction paper, yarn)

1. Cover three small cardboard boxes with glue and construction paper. Cut out a shape from each box. Decorate the boxes with markers or crayons.

2. Make a small hole in the top and bottom of two boxes. Make one hole in the third box.

3. Glue pieces of yarn in the holes to connect the boxes. Tie a loop at the top to hang the mobile.

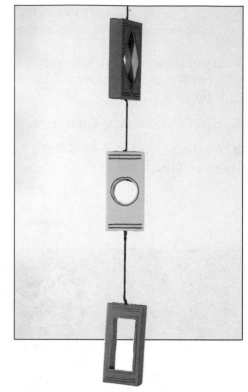

PENNY PAPERWEIGHT
(plastic jar lid, pennies, felt)

1. Glue pennies to the top of a plastic jar lid.

2. Cut a strip of felt and glue it around the edge of the lid.

BUTTON NAME PLAQUE
(heavy cardboard, fabric, rickrack, buttons, ribbon)

1. Cover a rectangular piece of heavy cardboard with glue and fabric. Add rickrack around the edges.

2. Print a name on the fabric. Squeeze glue on each letter and press buttons into the glue.

3. When dry, glue a piece of ribbon on the back for a hanger.

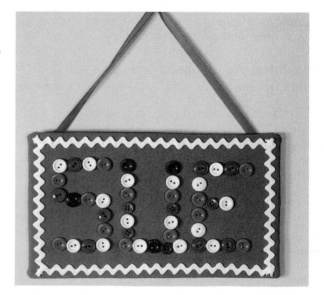

TRIANGLE PUPPY NOTE
(construction paper, marker)

1. Cut a piece of construction paper in half the long way.

2. Mark the center of the long side of one piece and draw lines from the center to each end of the other long side. Cut away the side pieces, leaving a long, thin triangle.

3. Turn the triangle so the tip is the puppy's nose. Fold two sides of the triangle down for its ears. Draw eyes and nose with a marker. Add spots.

4. Write a message on the back and send as a note to a friend.

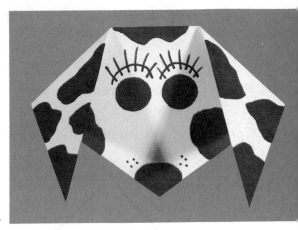

SCENTED KEEPSAKE
(lightweight cotton fabric, lace, rubber band, ribbon, potpourri of herbs, flowers, and spices)

1. Cut out two identical round circles, one from a piece of lightweight cotton fabric and the other from a piece of lace.

2. Place the cotton fabric right-side down on top of the lace. Pour a potpourri of herbs, flowers, and spices in the center of the circle.

3. Gather the cotton and lace around the potpourri and hold together tightly with a rubber band.

4. Tie a ribbon over the rubber band. Place the scented bag in a clothing drawer.

PAPIER-MÂCHÉ PHOTO FRAME
(corrugated cardboard, old newspaper or paper towels, flour and water, bowl, poster paint, lightweight cardboard, yarn)

1. Have an adult help you cut a picture frame shape from corrugated cardboard.

2. Cut small shapes from scrap cardboard and glue them on top of the frame to make a design.

3. To make papier-mâché, mix flour and water together in a bowl until it is the consistency of ketchup.

4. Tear small strips of newspaper or paper towels and dip them into the flour mixture. Place the strips on the frame, covering the edges and the back. Let dry for at least one day.

5. Paint the frame with several coats of poster paint. Let each coat dry before adding another one.

6. When finished, tape a photo in the frame. Place a sheet of lightweight cardboard over the back of the photo to protect it. Add a yarn hanger.

PAPER-PUNCH NOTE CARD
(paper)

1. Fold a sheet of 5-by-7-inch paper in half.

2. Punch out dots from colorful paper. Glue the dots to the front of the card.

3. Complete your designs with markers, colored pencils, or crayons.

FOUR SEASONS CLIPBOARD
(heavy cardboard, construction paper, two spring-type clothespins, string)

1. Cover a piece of heavy cardboard with light-colored construction paper.

2. Glue two spring-type clothespins at the top center of the board.

3. To decorate, cut and glue on four trees from brown paper. Add a few leaves to the first tree for spring, a green treetop to the second for summer, an orange treetop to the third for fall, and leave the last tree bare for winter.

4. Tape a piece of string to the back of the clipboard for a hanger.

CUBE PICTURE STORY
(poster board, crayons or markers)

1. Cut six pieces of poster board, each 6 inches square.

2. Think of a very short story. Number four squares of poster board 1 through 4. Draw a picture and write a sentence on each one for the story.

3. Lay the four squares side by side and tape them together, as shown. Pick up the taped squares and fold them to form a cube. Tape square 1 to square 4.

4. Put your story title on the fifth square, and tape it to the top. Tape the blank square to the bottom.

5. Share your story with friends and family.

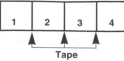

DESK ORGANIZER
(large cereal box, construction paper, several small boxes)

1. Cut away the front of a large cereal box. Cover the sides, inside and out, and the inside bottom of the box with glue and construction paper.

2. Arrange several small boxes inside the large box. Cover the small boxes with paper, and glue them into position. Let dry.

3. Place rubber bands, pencils, pens, and other supplies in the boxes.

GOURD ANIMAL
(small gourd, scrap cloth, acrylic paint, construction paper, metal washer)

1. Wash a small gourd, and polish the outer skin with a cloth.

2. With a pencil, draw the pattern of a penguin, goose, kangaroo, or other animal onto the gourd.

3. Paint the gourd with acrylic paint and let dry. Add features from construction paper.

4. Glue a metal washer about the size of a quarter to the bottom of the gourd so it will stand up.

TRIANGLE TOOTH FAIRY
(white paper, toothpick, large plastic cap, markers, cotton)

1. To make the Tooth Fairy's body, cut one large and two smaller triangles from white paper. Cut out a head and two hands. Glue the pieces together, as shown. Add a face and hair with markers.

2. To make a wand, attach a cut-paper or sticker star to the end of a toothpick. Glue it in the fairy's hand.

3. Decorate the outside of a large plastic cap. Place some cotton inside the cap so it will be a safe place to leave a tooth.

4. Glue the Tooth Fairy body behind the cap.

Back view

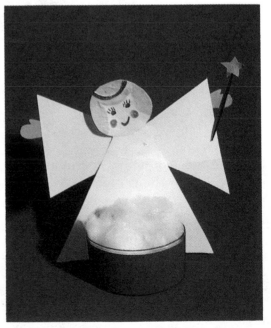

DOG RIBBON CADDY
(paper towel tube, corrugated cardboard, fabric, chenille stick, paper clips)

1. For the body, spread glue on a paper towel tube and cover it with fabric.

2. For the head and feet, cut front and back pieces from corrugated cardboard. Cover them with fabric and attach to the ends of the tube.

3. For the tail, poke a hole in the back piece and insert a chenille stick with some glue.

4. For the head of the dog, add features cut from fabric or paper. Wrap ribbons around the dog's body. Hold with paper clips.

HALF-GALLON BUS
(half-gallon milk carton, construction paper, stickers, cardboard, bottle tops)

1. Press down to flatten the top of a half-gallon milk carton. Tape to hold in place. Cover the carton with glue and construction paper.

2. Decorate the bus with paper and markers to make a sign and windows. Add stickers or draw on faces.

3. Draw and cut out wheels from cardboard. Paint them black. When they are dry, glue them to the bus. Glue on bottle tops for headlights.

BOX SCULPTURE
(corrugated cardboard, small cardboard boxes, poster paint, construction paper, yarn)

1. Use a piece of heavy corrugated cardboard for the base of the sculpture. Glue small cardboard boxes in a design on top and let dry.

2. Paint the boxes and the cardboard base. Decorate the boxes with paint or pieces of construction paper.

3. Glue a yarn loop hanger to the back.

BOOKWORM BOOKENDS
(two half-gallon juice or milk cartons, construction paper, rocks)

1. Cut two half-gallon juice or milk cartons in half and discard the tops.

2. Cover the carton halves with glue and paper. Draw a worm shape on paper. Add features with markers and cut out the worm.

3. Cut the worm in half. Glue the front part of the worm onto one bookend and print the word "BOOK" below it. Glue the back part of the worm onto the other bookend and print the word "WORM" below it.

4. Place rocks inside each bookend so they will be heavy enough to hold books in place.

SEWING KIT
(poster board, fabric, rickrack, felt)

1. Cut a piece of poster board for the cover of the sewing kit. Cover it with glue and fabric. Trim the edges and add rickrack. Fold in half and open.

2. Cut another piece of poster board and a piece of felt a little smaller than the cover. Cut parallel notches on each side of the poster board and wind thread through the notches.

3. Place the poster board of thread inside the cover. Place the felt on top. Turn all layers over so the outside of the cover is facing right-side up. Staple through all three layers at the fold.

4. Add needles, buttons, straight pins, and safety pins to the felt section of the sewing kit.

NEWSPAPER NELSON
(old newspaper, paper, yarn)

1. Use four sheets of newspaper for the front and four sheets of newspaper for the back of Newspaper Nelson. Fold other sheets of newspaper into long strips for his arms and legs.

2. Place the sheets of newspaper together and start stapling Nelson's body together at the edge. As you come to the places where arms and legs belong, insert them before stapling. Leave the whole top open for stuffing later.

3. Cut feet, hands, and facial features from paper. Staple or glue them in place.

4. Crumple sheets of newspaper and carefully stuff the body. Staple the top together, adding yarn for hair as you staple.

PATCHWORK TRIVET
(corrugated cardboard, fabric, cord)

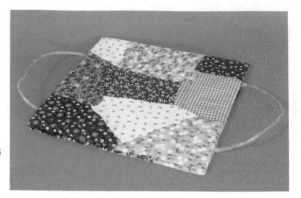

1. Cut two identical squares of corrugated cardboard.

2. Glue different shapes of fabric scraps to one side of each square, starting in a corner and wrapping the outside pieces of fabric over the edges of the cardboard to the back.

3. For the handles, cut two pieces of cord. Glue the handles to the back of one square.

4. Spread glue on the backs of both squares and press them together.

SLEEPY BEAR MITTEN HANGER
(plastic lid, two paper plates, construction paper, cotton, two plastic spring-type clothespins with holes, yarn)

1. Glue a plastic lid to the bottom of a paper plate for the bear's snout. Roll a strip of black construction paper and glue it to the snout.

2. To make the eyes, cut two rectangles of black paper. Then cut slits and curl them with a pencil for lashes. Glue them to the paper plate.

3. Make a hat from construction paper. Attach the hat with glue, adding some cotton for trim. Cut sections from another paper plate for the bear's ears and glue these on at the sides of the hat.

4. Punch two holes under the bear's chin. Cut two pieces of yarn, each about 20 inches long. Thread a clothespin onto each piece of yarn. Tie the yarn into a bow through the two holes.

5. Punch two holes behind the hat and thread a piece of yarn through them. Tie the ends in a bow for a hanger.

BOX FISH
(cereal box, construction paper, yarn)

1. Cut a long and a short corner from a cereal box.

2. Glue pieces of construction paper over the box corners and glue them together in a fish shape. Add features cut from paper.

3. Lightly tape a piece of yarn to the top of the fish so it will hang straight. Once you find the right spot, poke a hole through the top of the fish.

4. Glue the piece of yarn in the hole. Tie a loop at the other end of the yarn and hang the fish.

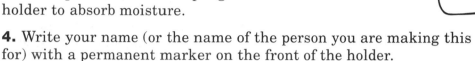

TOOTHBRUSH HOLDER
(white plastic dishwashing detergent bottle, cellulose sponge, permanent marker)

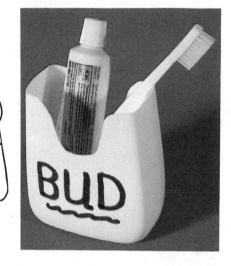

1. Have an adult help you cut off the top half of a plastic dishwashing detergent bottle. Wash and dry the bottom half. Discard the top.

2. Cut rounded sections from the front and the back of the bottle half to look like a big tooth, as shown. Poke small holes in the bottom for drainage.

3. Cut a piece of cellulose sponge to fit in the bottom of the holder to absorb moisture.

4. Write your name (or the name of the person you are making this for) with a permanent marker on the front of the holder.

SILHOUETTE, OR SHADOW PICTURE
(flashlight or slide projector, white and black construction paper, poster board, yarn)

1. In a dark room, place a lit flashlight or slide projector on a table. Lightly tape a piece of white construction paper to the wall right where the light is shining. Sit between the light and the paper, so that your profile falls on the paper. Move closer to or farther from the paper until the silhouette, or shadow, is the size you want.

2. Have a partner draw around your silhouette on the paper. Remove the paper from the wall and go over the outline, correcting any shaky lines.

3. Cut out the silhouette. Place it on a piece of black construction paper, trace around it, and cut it out.

4. Glue the black silhouette onto a piece of white paper. Mount the picture on a piece of poster board. Sign your name and the date. Add a piece of yarn to the back for a hanger.

PET PLACE MAT
(white poster board, construction paper, clear self-adhesive paper)

1. Cut a piece of white poster board large enough for your pet's food dishes.

2. Design a picture of your pet with markers and cutouts from construction paper. You could print your pet's name on part of the picture.

3. Cut two pieces of clear self-adhesive paper a little larger than the mat itself. (You may need an adult to help you separate the paper.) Cover the front and the back of the place mat. Trim the edges with scissors.

4. Keep the mat clean with a damp cloth.

PERKY PENGUIN
(uncooked egg, large sewing needle, bowl, cardboard, construction paper, 1-inch plastic foam ball)

1. Wash and dry an uncooked egg. Stick a large sewing needle into the pointed end of the egg, making sure to poke through the membrane under the shell. Turn the egg over, and stick the needle through the other end, making a larger hole than the first.

2. Over a bowl, blow through the small hole, allowing the inside of the egg to flow into the bowl. Carefully rinse the shell in cold water. (Use the egg for baking or scramble it for breakfast.)

3. Cut two large feet from cardboard in the shape shown, and cover them with construction paper. Glue the eggshell to the feet and let dry.

4. Paint the eggshell, making a penguin body. Glue a 1-inch plastic-foam ball to the top of the body for the head. Decorate with markers and paper.

SPRING BIRD'S HOME
(grass, leaves, twigs, flour, water, large plastic lid, miniature marshmallows, construction paper)

1. In a small bowl, mix together three tablespoons of water and three tablespoons of flour.

2. Place nesting material such as grass, leaves, and twigs on a large plastic lid. Pour half of the flour mixture over it and shape it into a nest.

3. Dip miniature marshmallows into some of the mixture, and place them inside the nest for eggs.

4. Decorate the nest with birds and flowers made from construction paper.

WOODEN PLAQUE
(twelve ice-cream sticks, old magazine or greeting card, yarn)

1. Spread a thin layer of glue on two ice-cream sticks. Place them, glue-side up, several inches apart. Position the remaining ice-cream sticks on top, as shown.

2. Cut a picture from an old magazine or greeting card, and glue it onto the sticks.

3. For a hanger, glue a piece of yarn to the back.

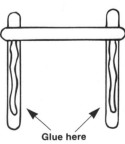

Glue here

DECORATED NOTE PAPER
(white or colored paper, rickrack, ribbon)

1. With a pencil, lightly sketch a design on a piece of white or colored paper.

2. Cut pieces of rickrack and ribbon to make the shapes you want. Arrange them on the sketch to make a design.

3. Use a little glue to attach them to the paper. Blot up any extra glue with a tissue.

4. When dry, use a marker to add such details as eyes, legs, stems, or leaves.

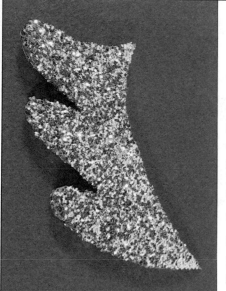

GLITTER PIN
(heavy cardboard, safety pin, glitter)

1. Cut a design from a piece of heavy cardboard.

2. Cover one side of the design with glue and sprinkle it with glitter. Let it dry thoroughly. Then shake off any excess glitter.

3. Tape or glue a safety pin to the back of the glittery design.

SCULPTURE FROM SCRAPS
(scraps of wood, nuts, bolts, washers, poster paint)

1. Stack various pieces of wood in interesting shapes.

2. Glue the wood pieces together. It may be necessary to let some sections dry before adding others to the sculpture.

3. Paint the wood sculpture, and glue on bolts and washers to add details.

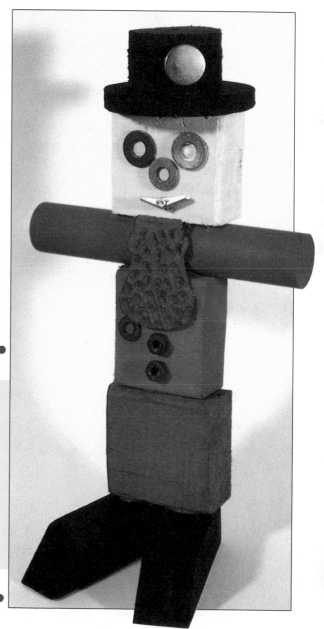

PUPPY PAPERWEIGHT
(small gelatin box, dried beans or stones, fabric, felt, ribbon)

1. Fill a gelatin box with stones or beans. Secure both ends of the box with tape.

2. Cover the box with fabric. Cut ears from felt and glue one on each side, attaching them only at the top so the ears can flop away from the head.

3. Add other features from felt. Add a ribbon collar.

TRAILER TRUCK
(cracker box, two pudding boxes, poster paint, construction paper, cardboard, bottle caps)

1. To make the trailer, tape the flaps on a cracker box shut. Tape two pudding boxes together for the cab. Cover the cab and the trailer with glue and construction paper.

2. Glue the trailer and the cab together. Draw and cut out wheels from cardboard. Paint them, then glue them to the truck.

3. Decorate with construction paper and markers. Roll a piece of paper into a tube and glue it to the side of the cab for an exhaust pipe.

4. Add bottle caps for headlights.

THE LOOK-AROUND CLOWN
(plastic drinking cup, plastic-foam ball, ice-cream stick, felt, rickrack, chenille stick)

1. Dip an ice-cream stick in glue and push it into the center of a plastic-foam ball.

2. Turn a plastic drinking cup upside down. Poke a hole in the center of the bottom of the cup, large enough so the stick can turn around.

3. Decorate the head and body with pieces of felt, rickrack, and chenille stick.

4. Put the ice-cream stick into the cup through the hole. By holding the stick with your hand inside the cup, you can move the clown's head up, down, and around.

JACK AND THE BEANSTALK

(one paper towel tube, four bathroom tissue tubes, construction paper, poster paint, yarn, paper clips, plastic drinking straw, cotton, ice-cream stick)

1. Paint a paper towel tube green and let it dry. Cut leaf shapes from construction paper and glue them to the tube. For the stem, glue a long piece of yarn around the leaves.

2. Glue together four bathroom tissue tubes to make a castle. Hold them together with paper clips until the glue dries. Cut sections from the castle towers. Paint the castle. Add a door and windows cut from paper.

3. Print "Giant" on a pennant made from paper. Glue it to a drinking straw. Place the pennant on top of the castle with glue.

4. Glue the beanstalk and castle together, holding with paper clips until the glue dries.

5. Place glue around the bottom of the castle and the beanstalk. Glue cotton in place to look like clouds.

6. Draw Jack on paper and staple him to a long piece of yarn twice the length of the beanstalk. Tie the other end of the yarn to an ice-cream stick.

7. Drop the stick down the beanstalk. When the stick comes out at the bottom, pull on the yarn and see Jack go up the beanstalk.

RAIN GAUGE

(clear plastic 35mm film canister, ice-cream stick, rubber band, permanent marker, clear nail polish)

1. Carefully measure from the bottom of a clear plastic 35mm film canister, drawing short lines every 1/4 inch with a permanent marker. Apply a coat of clear nail polish over the lines, making them waterproof.

2. Glue the canister to an ice-cream stick. Also attach a rubber band to help hold the canister in place.

3. Push the stick into the ground in an open space where there are no bushes or trees.

HANDY KEEPER

(food container with plastic lid, scrap wallpaper, old magazines)

1. Cover a food container with a scrap piece of wallpaper.

2. Paste on cartoons cut from old magazines.

3. Label the front of the container "Tiny Toys" or the name of whatever it will store.

YARN AND PLASTIC NECKLACE
(large plastic lid, yarn)

1. Cut around the edge of a large plastic lid, making a design.

2. With a paper punch, punch holes evenly around the edge of the lid. Gently fold the lid in half and punch a hole on the fold. Unfold. There should be one hole in the center of the lid.

3. Cut a long piece of yarn. Wrap one end with tape, making a point. Thread the yarn through the holes around the edges and through the center, making a design.

4. Glue the yarn ends on the back of the necklace. Glue one punched plastic dot in the center. Thread a long piece of yarn through one of the holes so you can wear it around your neck.

NIFTY PAGE MARKER
(old envelope)

1. Cut the bottom corner from an envelope, giving the edge a decorative shape.

2. Use crayons, markers, or paper cutouts to decorate the bookmark.

3. Slip the bookmark over the top corner of a page in your book to mark your place.

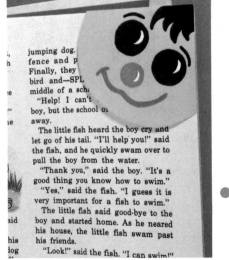

CATERPILLAR NAMEPLATE
(6-inch paper plates, paper punch, ribbon)

1. Use one paper plate for each letter of a first name plus one paper plate for the caterpillar's head.

2. Color the edges of the paper plates with markers. Draw one letter of the name in the center of each plate.

3. Decorate one paper plate as the caterpillar's head. Add paper antennae.

4. Place the paper plates in order. Punch a hole at the edge of each paper plate and join them with bows tied from ribbon.

5. To hang, punch a hole in the plate at each end and attach a ribbon loop.

BROOM FRIEND
(large brown paper bag, paint, paper, an old hat,
newspaper, broom, string, handkerchief)

1. Turn a large brown paper bag upside down, and paint a face on one side.

2. Cut strips of paper and glue them to the bag for hair. Glue on an old hat.

3. Fill the bag with crumpled newspaper. Place a broomstick into the center of the bag. Tie a piece of string tightly around the bottom of the bag. Tie a handkerchief over the string.

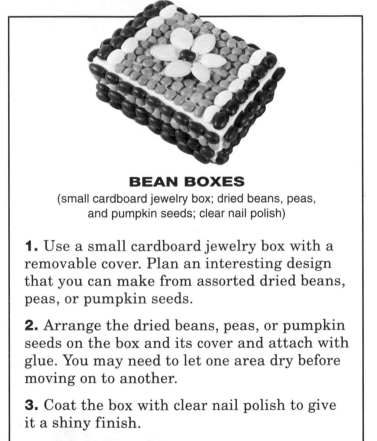

BEAN BOXES
(small cardboard jewelry box; dried beans, peas,
and pumpkin seeds; clear nail polish)

1. Use a small cardboard jewelry box with a removable cover. Plan an interesting design that you can make from assorted dried beans, peas, or pumpkin seeds.

2. Arrange the dried beans, peas, or pumpkin seeds on the box and its cover and attach with glue. You may need to let one area dry before moving on to another.

3. Coat the box with clear nail polish to give it a shiny finish.

RACING CARS
(wooden clothespins, poster paint, poster board, paper)

1. Cover clothespins with poster paint for the car bodies. Cut wheels from poster board and glue them to the clothespins.

2. Draw drivers on paper, cut them out, and glue them in the slots of the clothespins.

FREE-FORM ART
(water and white glue, plastic bowl, construction paper, watercolors, felt-tipped pen)

1. Mix a solution of one part white glue and one part water in a small plastic bowl. Brush the solution onto a piece of construction paper.

2. While the paper is still wet, press the tip of a paintbrush filled with watercolor onto your paper to create each flower.

3. When the paint is dry, outline the flowers with ink or a felt-tipped pen.

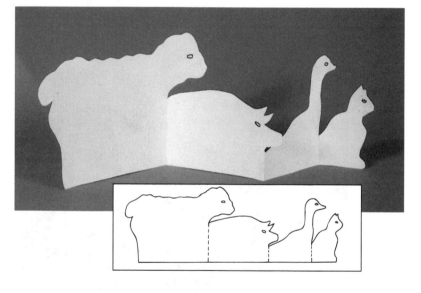

ANIMAL NOTE CARD
(paper)

1. On paper, draw side views, or profiles, of animals all in a row.

2. At each place where a new animal begins, draw a dotted line to the bottom of the paper.

3. Fold back and forth along the dotted lines. Unfold and cut around the solid lines of the animals, as shown. When unfolded, the card will stand up.

4. Write a message on the back of the card.

PARKING GARAGE
(cardboard box with flap, white paper, crayons, paints or markers)

1. Find a cardboard box with one big flap that can be used as the opening of the building.

2. Glue a piece of white paper to the front of the flap. Use crayons, paints, or markers to draw designs, such as bricks or siding, on the flap, making it look like the front of a parking garage.

3. Continue the design around the rest of the box.

4. Store toy cars, trucks, and other playthings in the storage-box building.

BIRDHOUSE WALL DECORATION

(plastic-foam tray, fabric, ribbon, rickrack, construction paper, yarn)

1. Draw a house shape on a large plastic-foam tray. Draw a separate roof shape for the house, as shown. Cut out the two shapes.

2. Wrap fabric over the house, taping the fabric to the back. Do the same with the roof. Then glue the roof to the house.

3. Add ribbon and rickrack to trim the roof. Cut and glue pieces of construction paper for the bird, door, and flowers.

4. To hang the decoration, glue a piece of yarn on the back. Glue paper on the back to cover the taped fabric.

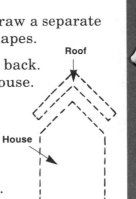

Roof

House

POMPON PET

(yarn, cardboard, felt)

1. Wrap yarn around a 3-inch square of cardboard. (The more yarn you wind, the fluffier the pet will be.)

2. Carefully slip the yarn from the cardboard and tie a small piece of yarn tightly around the center, as shown.

3. Cut through all the loops, and fluff up the yarn. Cut features from felt, and attach them with glue.

Wrap yarn

Tie around center

Cut loops

BIG BEAR BANK

(cardboard container with plastic lid, felt, yarn)

1. Place a plastic lid from a cardboard container on a piece of felt. Trace around the lid twice, making two circles. Cut out the felt circles and glue one to the lid and one to the bottom of the container.

2. Cut out felt ears and glue them just under the edge of the felt circle on the lid. Cut other facial features from felt and glue them in place. Add a small tail to the other end.

3. Have an adult help you cut a slit in the side of the container, large enough to slip money through.

4. Brush a 1/2-inch strip of glue on one edge of the container. Press yarn pulled from a ball or skein into the glue, and wind the yarn around the container until it is covered. Glue the end in place. When dry, cut away the yarn to uncover the slit.

5. Cut out cardboard feet and cover them with felt. Trim around the edges with scissors. Add felt claws. Glue the feet to the container to keep it from rolling.

MAKEUP HOLDER
(three quart-size milk cartons, white glue and water, paintbrush, bowl, fabric, spring-type clothespins, rubber bands, ribbon)

1. Measure 3 inches from the bottom of three quart-size milk cartons. Cut off the tops of the cartons and discard.

2. Cut three strips of fabric, each 4 inches wide and 12 inches long. Mix white glue and a little water together in a bowl.

3. Brush the glue mixture on one side of a carton. Press one strip of fabric into the glue with the top edges even. Continue around the other three sides. Glue the excess fabric to the bottom. Repeat with the other two cartons.

4. Place the cartons side by side and glue them together. Hold the centers together with spring-type clothespins. Place a rubber band around the bottoms.

5. When dry, remove the rubber band and clothespins. Add a piece of ribbon and a bow. Place makeup and hair care items in the holder.

DOORKNOB SIGNS
(graph paper, thin yarn, plastic drinking straw, markers)

1. On a piece of graph paper about 6 inches wide and 9 inches long, form letters by coloring in the squares with markers. Spell out a message.

2. Cut a piece of thin yarn approximately 20 inches long.

3. Tightly wrap a small piece of tape around one end of the yarn, and thread the yarn through a straw. Then cut the tape off the yarn and tie the ends together.

4. Fold the top of the graph paper over the straw, and tape it to the back. Hang the sign on a doorknob.

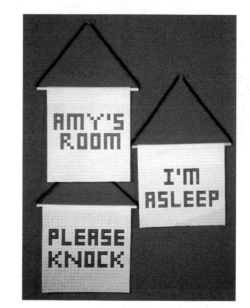

TABLE TURTLE
(smooth round rock, poster board, poster paint)

1. Find a smooth round rock. Wash it and let dry.

2. Draw a turtle shape, larger than the rock, on a piece of poster board. Cut out the turtle shape, cover it with green paint, and let dry.

3. Glue the rock to the turtle shape. Then paint the rock green. Using black paint, add details to the shell and head of the turtle.

4. Use as a paperweight or table decoration.

STAND-UP PICTURE FRAMES
(small box with lid, fabric, pictures or photos, poster board)

1. Cover a small box and lid with spots of glue. Press fabric into the glue, covering the entire box and overlapping the fabric to the inside.

2. Cut two pieces of poster board that will fit snugly into the boxes. Glue a picture to each one. Cut strips of fabric and glue them around the pictures as trim. Glue pictures to the inside.

3. To join the box and lid, cut two small pieces of fabric and glue them to each box, making hinges. When the glue is dry, stand the boxes up.

STACKING CONE FAMILY
(white poster board, markers, string)

1. Cut out a small, a medium, and a large circle from white poster board. Cut a slit to the center of each circle and pull one edge of the poster board over the other edge to form a cone shape. Tape along the seam edges.

2. Create faces with markers.

3. Tie a knot near the bottom of a long piece of string and thread the string through the smallest cone.

4. With the smallest cone resting on top of the first knot, tie another knot a few inches higher, and thread the medium cone. Repeat for the large cone.

5. Tape the string inside each cone to keep it from slipping. Knot a loop at the very top of the string.

6. Stack the cones with the biggest on top. As you lift the string, each smaller cone will appear. Hang it as a decoration, or play with it as a stacking toy.

"ME, MYSELF, AND I" BODY COLLAGE
(two large brown paper bags, old magazines, yarn)

1. Cut open two large brown paper bags. Tape the ends together to make one long piece of paper, a little longer and a little wider than yourself.

2. Carefully lie down on the paper, making sure all of you is inside the edges. Ask a partner to trace around you with a pencil. Cut out the body shape.

3. Cut out pictures of things you like from old magazines. Glue them to the body shape.

4. Attach a loop of yarn to the top to hang the collage on a door.

ROBOT

(plastic-foam cup, 1 1/2-inch plastic-foam ball, table knife, toothpicks, chenille stick, thread spool, paper)

1. Use a plastic-foam cup for the robot's body.

2. For the head, cut a 1 1/2-inch plastic-foam ball in half with a table knife and glue one half to the bottom of the cup. Cut the remaining piece of ball into quarters, and press two of the pieces on ends of toothpicks. Insert them into the head for antenae.

3. To make the wheel, thread a chenille stick through the sides of the cup and through a thread spool so that the spool extends just a little above the rim of the cup, as shown. Bend the ends of the chenille stick to form arms. Press two of the quartered foam pieces onto the ends of the arms.

4. Add cut-paper features to decorate the robot. A gentle push from the back moves the robot along a smooth surface.

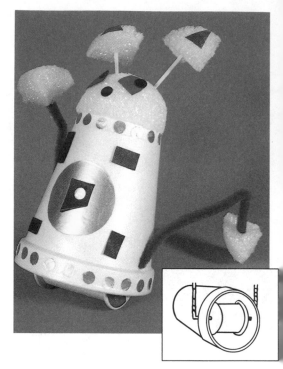

VAN

(elbow-macaroni cardboard box, construction paper, cardboard)

1. Cut a small section from an elbow-macaroni box, as shown. Cover the box with construction paper.

2. Draw and cut out wheels from cardboard. Glue the wheels on each side of the van.

3. Decorate the van with paper and markers.

BOOKWORM

(ice-cream stick, poster paint, pompon, marker, chenille stick, moveable plastic eyes)

1. Paint an ice-cream stick with poster paint and let dry.

2. Glue a pompon at one end for the head. Add other details to the ice-cream stick with a marker.

3. Cut a small piece of chenille stick. Bend it in the shape of antenae and glue it to the head. Glue on moveable plastic eyes.

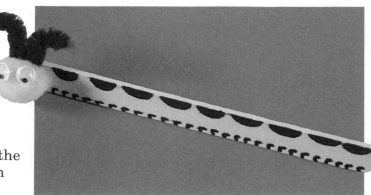

PLASTIC BOTTLE PENCIL HOLDER
(plastic detergent bottle, yarn, ribbon, construction paper)

1. Soak the detergent bottle in warm water to help soften the plastic and to remove the label. Then cut off the top half, leaving an oval-shaped piece attached to the back for the head.

2. Decorate the holder with paper and markers.

3. Make braided hair from yarn. To braid, cut three pieces of yarn the same length. Line up the pieces, and tie them together into a knot about 1 inch from one end. Braid by folding A over B and then C over A. Continue until the yarn is braided. Tie the ends into a knot again about 1 inch from the end. Glue the braid in place and tie a ribbon on each end.

FRAMED DOODLE DESIGN
(construction paper, poster board, yarn, permanent markers, paints, or crayons)

1. Use permanent markers to doodle lines onto a piece of construction paper.

2. Fill in the spaces with colors, using permanent markers, paints, or crayons.

3. To make a frame, cut four strips of poster board, each about 1 inch wide. Cut two for the length and two for the width, making each 1 inch longer than the picture.

4. Glue the long pair of strips in place over the front of the picture's edge. Then glue the shorter pair of strips in place. Make all four corners even.

5. Glue a piece of yarn to the back of the frame for a hanger.

PIE PAN TAMBOURINE
(two 8-inch aluminum pie pans, plastic- or paper-coated twist-ties)

1. Poke eight holes, 1 to 2 inches apart, just inside the rim of an 8-inch aluminum pie pan.

2. Cut small circles from the other aluminum pie pan for jangles. Punch a small hole in each one.

3. Using twist-ties, attach the jangles by twisting the ties at the very ends, so the jangles will hang loosely. Leave a space where there are no holes so you can hold the tambourine.

SEASHELL PLANTER
(small plastic bottle, sand, seashells)

1. Soak a small plastic bottle in warm water to make it easier to cut and to remove the label. Using scissors, cut away the top section.

2. Glue seashells onto the bottle in a pattern and let them dry.

3. Spread glue over the rest of the bottle, and sprinkle it with sand. Gently press the sand into the glue to help it stick.

CARDBOARD CAMERA
(tape, cereal box, construction paper,
gift-wrap tube, paper)

1. Secure the ends of a cereal box with tape. Cover the box with construction paper.

2. Cut a gift-wrap tube in half and cover it with paper. Cut a hole in each narrow side of the box, near the top, large enough to slide the tube through.

3. Decorate the camera with paper and draw meters, dials, and switches.

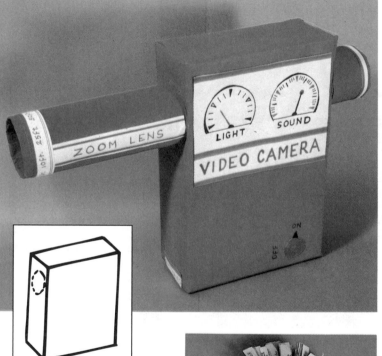

NEWSPAPER PUPPET
(newspaper, white paper)

1. You will need six pieces of newspaper, each 11 by 14 inches.

2. Roll five pieces together lengthwise, then wrap the sixth piece around them and tape together.

3. Make 3-inch cuts at one end, about 1/2 inch apart, for the hair. On white paper, draw features with markers and glue them in place.

PENNANTS
(felt or cloth)

1. Cut a pennant shape from felt or cloth.

2. Make letters that spell a short word or form initials. Glue these to the pennant along with other designs you cut out.

3. Hang the pennant in your room.

TORTOISE AND HARE RACERS
(walnut-shell halves, marbles, felt)

1. Use half of a walnut shell for each body. Remove the meat inside the shell.

2. Cut out heads and legs from felt. Glue them to the bodies.

3. Place a marble under each shell. The animals will race down a smooth slope, such as a board or box lid.

PRINT ART
(plastic-foam tray, pencil, tempera paint, construction paper)

1. Wash and dry a plastic-foam tray. Using a pencil, draw a picture on the inside of the tray. Make sure you press hard enough so that the lines are indented.

2. Brush a thin coat of tempera paint across the whole picture. Place a piece of construction paper on the painted surface, and rub your finger over the paper.

3. Carefully lift the paper from the tray, and let the painting dry.

4. Wash any remaining paint from the tray, and let dry. You can repeat this process with other colors of paint and paper.

WALLPAPER-COVERED WASTEBASKET

(large, round cardboard ice-cream container, scrap wallpaper, gift wrap, or fabric)

1. Glue scrap wallpaper, fancy gift wrap, or fabric to the outside of a cardboard container.

2. Decorate the outside with paper cutouts.

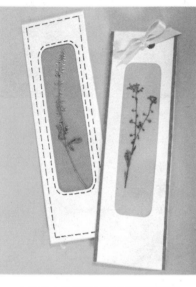

NATURE BOOKMARKS

(flowers, weeds, leaves, paper towels,
large book, construction paper, old window envelope, ribbon)

1. Place cuttings of flowers, weeds, or leaves between paper towels. Press them between the pages of a large book. Keep them in the book three to seven days to dry.

2. Following the diagram, cut a section from an old window envelope. Cut a piece of construction paper a little smaller than the cut section.

3. Glue the pressed plants on the paper, and place them in the envelope section so they will show through the window.

4. Seal the edges with glue. Decorate with markers, or punch two holes in the top and tie a ribbon through the holes.

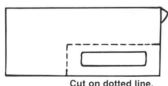

Cut on dotted line.

THINGS-I-WANT-TO-SAVE BOOK

(eight plastic sandwich bags, scrap wallpaper, yarn)

1. Stack about eight plastic sandwich bags together with the openings all at one end. Cut two pieces of scrap wallpaper slightly larger than the size of the sandwich bags.

2. Place the bags between the two pieces of wallpaper. Hold these together, and punch two holes at the closed ends of the bags.

3. Thread a piece of yarn through each hole, and tie the ends together in a bow.

4. Make a label from a piece of paper, and print "Things I Want to Save" on it. Glue the label to the cover.

5. Save postcards or other items in your book. During the year, you can look over what you have collected.

HAIR-CLIP HOLDER
(corrugated cardboard, 10-inch dinner plate,
poster paint, yarn, fabric)

1. Place a 10-inch dinner plate on a piece of corrugated cardboard and trace around it. Cut out the circle.

2. Cut out a section, as shown. This will be the top of the head where the hair clips are attached.

3. Paint part of the cardboard to look like a face. Paint around the cutout area, using a color to match the yarn you plan to use for hair.

4. Cut pieces of yarn for hair. Fold them in half and glue them as loops around the face. Add paper features. Add a fabric bow below the chin.

5. Punch a hole in the center at the top. Tie a piece of yarn for a hanger. Attach hair clips to the holder.

cut out

KITTY PLAYHOUSE
(large corrugated cardboard box, construction paper, string,
fabric, thread spools)

1. Find a large, 2-foot-deep corrugated cardboard box.

2. Turn the box over so the bottom faces up. Cut a door on one side of the box. Glue or staple a fabric flap over the door.

3. Cut out circles, squares, and triangles from the sides of the box.

4. Tie string to thread spools or other toys and hang them from the inside of the playhouse roof.

BUTTON-NOSE CLOWN
(felt, yarn)

1. Cut out a circle from felt. In the center of the circle, cut a slit that is large enough for a shirt button to go through.

2. Glue on pieces of yarn and felt to make a clown face, hair, and hat. Do not give the clown a nose.

3. Button the clown to your shirt through the slit in its face. The button will be the clown's nose.

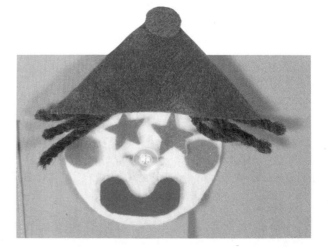

MINIATURE CASTLE
(construction paper, cardboard box)

1. Remove the lid from a small cardboard box. Glue construction paper to the outside of the box and let dry.

2. Use crayons or markers to sketch in a drawbridge and windows.

3. Cut teeth, or castle turrets, along one side of four strips of construction paper. Glue the strips around the top edge of the inside of the box.

4. Cut turrets along one side of four sheets of 8 1/2-by-11-inch paper. Add windows and doors with crayons or markers.

5. Roll each sheet into a tube, and glue or tape it closed. Glue the four rolls to the corners of the castle.

MAGNET MAZE
(8-inch paper plate, lightweight cardboard, magnetic strip, ice-cream stick)

1. On a paper plate, use markers or crayons to draw a circular maze. Draw a moon in the center. The starting point, or "Launch Pad," should be at the edge of the plate, and the finish should be in the center at the "Moon."

2. From lightweight cardboard, cut out the shape of a rocket, about the size of a quarter, and decorate it. Glue the rocket to a small magnet cut from a magnetic strip. Glue another small magnet to the end of an ice-cream stick. (Make sure you glue the right side of the magnet up—that is, the side that will attract, rather than repel, the other magnet when the two are placed back to back.)

3. Hold the magnetic stick under the plate, and guide your rocket from the launch pad to the moon.

PEN AND PENCIL HOLDER
(old magazines, pencil, paper clips, round cardboard container, construction paper)

1. Remove colorful pages from an old magazine. Lay a pencil at one edge of a page. Brush a thin line of glue at the other edge of the page. Roll the page around the pencil and press the glued edge into place.

2. Pull the pencil out of the tube. If the glue is not quite dry, slip paper clips onto the ends of the tube to hold the paper in place.

3. Use a round cardboard container, like the kind peanuts come in, for the holder. Cut the tubes the same height as the container. Brush glue on the seam of each tube, and glue the tubes onto the container. Have enough tubes handy to cover the entire container.

4. Cut and glue strips of construction paper to decorate the top and the bottom of the holder.

LION PUPPET
(small brown paper bag, construction paper)

1. To make the lion's head, draw and cut out from construction paper a head and ears about the same width as the bottom of the paper bag. Add eyes, a nose, a mouth, and whiskers.

2. Glue the lion's head to the center of a sheet of paper. Cut 2 to 3 inches away from the lion's head to make the mane. Then cut slits around the edges, and use a pencil to curl the fringe a little. Glue the lion's head to the bottom of the paper bag.

3. To make the body, draw and cut out a piece of paper and glue it to the front of the bag just under the lion's head. Add two paper feet.

4. Place your hand inside the bag and curve your fingers over the fold to move the lion's head.

MIXED-UP CHARACTER MOBILE
(lightweight cardboard, crayons or markers, string)

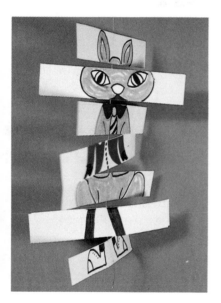

1. On two pieces of lightweight cardboard, draw six or seven horizontal lines about an inch apart.

2. On each piece of cardboard, draw a picture of a different character. Start with the head within the first two lines. Cut the pictures apart along the horizontal lines.

3. Lay the strips of one picture facedown, leaving small spaces between the strips. Apply glue to the backs of these strips and lay a piece of string in the center, leaving extra string at the top for a hanger.

4. Glue each piece of the second picture faceup on top of the pieces of the first picture. Be sure to keep the pieces in the correct order.

EGG-CARTON CATERPILLAR
(cardboard egg carton, poster paint, construction paper)

1. Cut through the center section of a cardboard egg carton, making the long six-cup section the body of the caterpillar. Make the legs by cutting a small section from both sides of the cups.

2. Paint the outside with green paint. Glue the body to a piece of black paper. Trim around the edge when dry.

3. Cut the head from green paper and draw on features with a marker. Make the antennae from black paper and glue them to the head.

A HAPPY FAMILY
(old stockings, cotton balls, yarn, cardboard, felt)

1. Wash and dry a pair of old stockings. Cut out three sections, each a different length.

2. Tie a knot at one end of each section. Turn the sections inside out, and stuff them with cotton. When they are full, tie knots to close them.

3. Glue on scraps of felt, yarn, and cotton to create the faces.

4. Cut three squares of cardboard for bases, and cover them with felt cut the same size.

5. Glue a happy family member on top of each base.

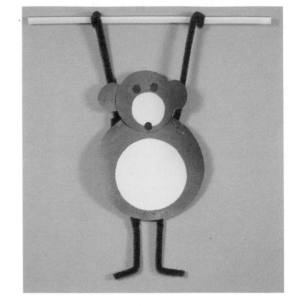

TWIRLING MONKEY
(construction paper, chenille sticks, plastic drinking straw)

1. Draw and cut out circles from construction paper. Glue these together to make the monkey.

2. Staple pieces of chenille sticks to the monkey for the arms and the legs.

3. Wrap the ends of the arms around a plastic drinking straw.

4. Hold the straw in your hand, and swing the monkey around the straw.

BOX BIRDS
(small cardboard box, construction paper, poster board, 3-inch plastic-foam ball,
table knife, wooden or plastic stir sticks)

1. Cover a small cardboard box with construction paper. Cut out a head, wings, and a tail from poster board. Decorate with markers or crayons and glue the body parts in place.

2. Cut a 3-inch plastic-foam ball in half with a table knife. Color one half with a marker. Save the other half for another bird.

3. Poke stir sticks into the bottom of the box for legs and add glue. Let dry. Push the legs into the plastic-foam ball half and add glue.

4. Cut feet from paper and glue them to the ball.

BINOCULARS
(two 5-inch cardboard tubes, construction paper, wood or heavy cardboard, yarn)

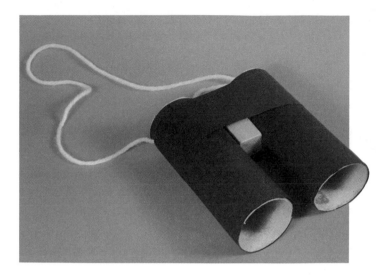

1. Cover two 5-inch cardboard tubes with construction paper. Glue a piece of wood or heavy cardboard between the tubes to separate them enough to fit your eyes.

2. Cut a strip of paper about 1 1/2 inches wide and long enough to go around both tubes. Glue this strip around the tubes at the viewing end.

3. To attach a strap, paper punch a hole in each side of the binoculars, thread a piece of yarn through, and tie a knot at each end.

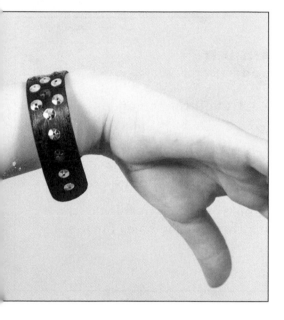

TONGUE DEPRESSOR BRACELET
(wooden tongue depressor, warm water, frozen-juice container, rubber bands, poster paint, sequins, clear nail polish)

1. Soak a wooden tongue depressor in warm water about an hour or until you can gently bend it around a frozen-juice container.

2. Once it is around the container, place rubber bands on top of the tongue depressor to hold it in place. Let dry for one day.

3. Remove the tongue depressor, cover it with poster paint, and let dry. Glue sequins around the outside. When dry, cover with clear nail polish.

WINDOW VEGETABLE GARDEN
(cardboard, plastic wrap, white glue, yarn, food coloring, paper plate)

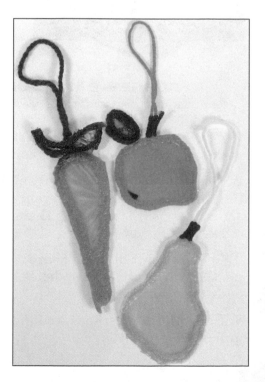

1. Draw the outlines of vegetables on a piece of cardboard. Cover with plastic wrap. Squeeze white glue on the outline of each vegetable. Press two strands of yarn into the glue.

2. On a paper plate, mix a few drops of food coloring with white glue. Pour the colored glue inside the vegetable outline. Make a loop of yarn for a hanger. Dry for several days.

3. Peel the vegetables from the plastic wrap and hang them in the window.

DOG BISCUIT CARD
(poster board, dog bone-shaped biscuit)

1. Fold a piece of 5-by-10-inch poster board in half to form a card.

2. Open the card. Place a dog bone-shaped biscuit on the front and trace around it. Cut out the bone shape and fold the card.

3. On the panel directly behind the cutout, glue the dog biscuit in place. Close the card. The dog biscuit should pop through the opening.

4. On the front of the card write "A Wish...", and inside the card write "of happiness with your new puppy."

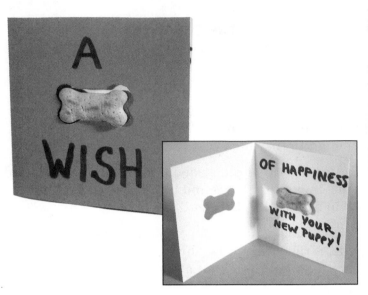

CAR CARRIER
(half-gallon milk carton, old magazines, yarn)

1. Wash a half-gallon milk carton. Cut off the top and discard it.

2. Cut out lots of pictures of cars, trucks, planes, and boats from old magazines and glue them all over the outside of the milk carton.

3. Use a paper punch to punch a hole on opposite sides of the carton near the top edge. Tie yarn through the holes for a handle.

RUBBER-BAND BULLETIN BOARD
(corrugated cardboard, shelf paper or wrapping paper, rubber bands, yarn)

1. Cover a 10-by-12-inch piece of corrugated cardboard with brightly colored self-adhesive shelf paper or gift wrap.

2. Use scissors to cut several small slits along each side of the cardboard. Stretch different-colored rubber bands across the board, inserting them in the slits, to make a criss-cross design.

3. To hang your bulletin board, make a loop by threading a piece of yarn through two holes at the top and tying the ends together.

4. Slide phone messages, reminders, and photographs under the rubber bands.

THE MOUSE AND THE CHEESE
(cellulose sponge, Brazil nut, construction paper, felt, ribbon)

1. Cut a small triangle from a cellulose sponge. Glue a Brazil nut on top.

2. From black felt, cut two large teardrop shapes for the ears and a small strip for the tail. Glue these to the nut.

3. To make the eyes, paper-punch two white dots and draw a black dot in the center of each. Glue these in place.

4. Tie a small ribbon into a bow, and glue it between the nut and the sponge.

TISSUE SNOWMAN
(construction paper, white facial tissues)

1. On a sheet of construction paper, draw an outline of a snowman.

2. Tear narrow strips from the long edge of white facial tissues, and then tear each strip apart in the middle.

3. Crumple the tissue strips into small wads. Spread glue on the snowman, and place the wads on the snowman until his entire body is covered.

4. Cut out a hat, eyes, and other details from paper and glue them on the snowman.

5. Add snow around the base of the snowman by gluing down more tissue wads.

COOKIE TRAY
(7-inch paper plate, 10-inch lace-paper doily, poster board)

1. Glue a 10-inch lace-paper doily in the center of a 7-inch paper plate.

2. Cut a 1-inch strip of poster board. Staple the ends to the paper plate, making a handle. Decorate with pieces cut from another doily.

3. Place cookies on the tray and serve them to your family or friends.

SPOOL DOLLS

(thread spools, paint, fabric, felt, 1-inch plastic-foam balls, buttons, sequins, rickrack, ribbon, pompons)

1. Decorate a spool with paint or scraps of fabric. Glue a small 1-inch plastic-foam ball to one end for the head.

2. Use colored yarn for hair and scraps of felt or fabric for the nose, mouth, and eyes.

3. Buttons, sequins, rickrack, yarn, and pompons can be glued on the spool to make many different kinds of spool dolls.

STAMP-AND-STICKER SAVER

(cardboard food container with plastic lid, stamps or stickers)

1. Use a clean, empty cardboard container that has a plastic lid.

2. Attach stamps or stickers to the outside of the container. Overlap some so that all the spaces are covered.

3. Save other stamps or stickers that you collect and place them inside the container.

PINCUSHION AND SCISSOR HOLDER

(frozen-juice container, toothpaste box, fabric, ribbon, cotton balls)

1. For the pincushion, cut a frozen-juice container in half. For the scissor holder, cut a large toothpaste box in half. Discard the top halves.

2. Cover the box and the container with glue and press fabric all the way around them, overlapping the fabric onto the inside edges. Add some ribbon for decoration.

3. Fill the pincushion with cotton balls. Cover the cotton with a piece of fabric, and glue it into the box.

4. Glue the pincushion and scissor holder together.

EASY STRING ART
(lightweight cardboard, yarn of different colors)

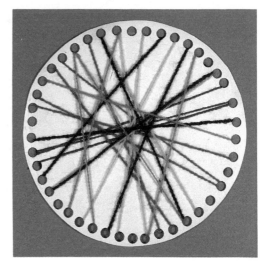

1. Cut out a simple shape, like a circle, from lightweight cardboard. Carefully paper-punch holes all around the edges of the shape.

2. Cut a long piece of yarn, and tape one end to the back of the cardboard. Thread the other end of the yarn up through a hole, across the front of the cardboard, and down into another hole.

3. Pull the yarn across the back of the cardboard, thread it up through another hole, and stretch it again across the front of the cardboard.

4. Continue to do this until you use up all the yarn. Tape the end to the back of the cardboard.

5. Pick another piece of yarn, of a different color, and repeat steps 2, 3, and 4. Attach a yarn loop at the top, and hang your piece of art.

TERRYCLOTH DOG
(terrycloth washcloth, felt, buttons, thread, string, ribbon)

1. Roll opposite sides of a terrycloth facecloth toward the center until they meet. Keeping the rolled sides together, fold down the ends evenly, forming two corners to make the legs.

2. Tie string snugly around each corner to form the head and the rear of the dog.

3. Cut and sew felt ears, a tail, and a tongue to the dog. Sew on button eyes and a nose. Sew on thread for whiskers.

4. Tie a ribbon around the dog's neck.

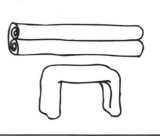

BILLY BUG
(12-inch paper towel tube, poster paint, paper, yarn, felt)

1. Cover a 12-inch paper towel tube with poster paint and let dry.

2. Cut six 2-inch lengths from the paper towel tube. Using a paper punch, punch holes opposite each other and on each end in four tubes. Tie them together loosely with yarn to form the middle of the bug's body.

3. Punch holes at one end only in the remaining two tubes. Attach one to the body for the head and attach the other for the tail.

4. Decorate with cutout paper and felt. Attach a yarn tail.

CRAWL-ALONG ALLIGATOR

(rectangular tissue box, green construction paper,
two 1-inch plastic-foam balls, chenille stick, thread spool)

1. Cut wedge shapes from two sides of a rectangular tissue box. Make one wedge shape longer than the other, as shown.

2. Cover the shapes with green construction paper. Glue the square ends of the wedges together.

3. To make the alligator's eyes, glue construction paper and 1-inch plastic-foam balls on the shorter wedge shape.

4. Cut and glue construction paper for the mouth, teeth, and nose. Thread a piece of chenille stick through a thread spool to use as a wheel and axle.

5. Poke a hole on each side of the larger wedge so that the wheel is positioned to allow the alligator to roll along.

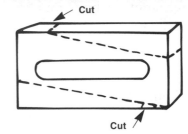

CLOWN STICK PUPPET

(plastic detergent bottle, yarn, construction paper,
cotton, wooden dowel)

1. Soak the label off a plastic detergent bottle and dry. Turn the bottle upside down and glue pieces of yarn to the bottle for hair.

2. To make the handle, soak a wad of cotton in a mixture of white glue and water. Wrap enough of the cotton around the end of a wooden stick so that the stick will fit tightly into the spout of the bottle. The soaked cotton will dry and hold the stick in place.

3. Glue on pieces of construction paper for the facial features. Add a paper bow tie.

SHELL AND STONE WREATH

(heavy cardboard, seashells, stones, yarn or string)

1. Cut a doughnut shape from a piece of heavy cardboard for the base of the wreath.

2. Glue colorful seashells and stones onto the cardboard.

3. Glue yarn or string to the back of the wreath for a hanger.

KITTEN BANK
(cardboard pudding box, felt, paper, cardboard)

1. Trim the side flaps at the open end of a cardboard pudding box so they are shaped like kitten ears. Glue pink felt to the inside of the ears.

2. Tape the other flaps shut. Cover the rest of the box with felt. Cut a coin slit in the top.

3. Cut eyes, a nose, and a mouth from felt and glue in place. Add whiskers made from strips of paper.

4. Cut a cardboard tail and cover it with felt. Glue the tail to the bottom of the kitten's body.

JUICE-LID WIND CHIMES
(two ice-cream sticks, yarn, sixteen frozen-juice lids)

1. Glue two ice-cream sticks together at their centers to form an X. Tie a piece of yarn at the X to help hold the sticks together and to make a loop for hanging.

2. Wash and dry sixteen frozen-juice lids. Cut four 1-foot pieces of yarn and a fifth piece 1 1/2 feet long.

3. Using three lids, glue one of the lids to the end of a piece of yarn, another one almost at the center, and the last one near the top, leaving about 3 inches of yarn. Repeat this three more times. Tie each piece of yarn to an end of one of the sticks.

4. Glue the remaining four lids onto the 1 1/2-foot length of yarn, leaving about 2 1/2 inches to be tied to the center of the sticks.

HALF AND HALF
(construction paper, markers)

1. Fold a piece of construction paper in half. Draw part of a head on one half of the paper, using a dark-colored marker. (Be sure to draw your lines to the edge of the fold.)

2. Turn the folded paper over and place it against a windowpane so the blank half is facing you.

3. If you look closely, you can see the lines you drew underneath. Trace over the lines, completing the head.

4. Finish the picture with colored markers.

PLASTIC-BOTTLE CAR
(two plastic detergent bottles, poster board, construction paper)

1. Soak the labels from two plastic detergent bottles and dry the bottles. Use one for the body of the car.

2. To make the cab of the car, cut the other bottle about 2 inches from the bottom and discard the top. Glue the bottom piece onto the body of the car.

3. Cut wheels from poster board and glue them onto the body. Add other features with construction paper.

ROLLERO GAME
(two bathroom tissue tubes, construction paper, plastic drinking straw)

1. Cover two bathroom tissue tubes with glue and construction paper. Let dry.

2. With a pencil, mark off 1 1/2 inches along each tube. Cut the tubes at the 1 1/2-inch marks. Decorate the tubes with stripes of different-colored paper for each player.

3. Set a starting point and a finish line on the table or floor. Race to the finish line by blowing through a plastic drinking straw to move your Rollero along.

BEAN BUG
(fabric, needle and thread, felt, dried beans or macaroni)

1. From fabric, cut two bug shapes about 6 inches long. From a contrasting fabric, cut a head shape to fit over the end of one bug piece and sew it in place.

2. With right sides together, sew almost all the way around the bug shapes. Turn the piece inside out and stuff it loosely with dried beans or small macaroni. Finish sewing.

3. Cut eyes and other details from felt or fabric. Sew them on.

4. Use the bug for a beanbag or a paperweight.

STICK MASK

(8-inch heavy paper plate, construction paper, markers or paint, lightweight cardboard, masking tape, ruler)

1. Have an adult help you cut two eyeholes in an 8-inch heavy paper plate. Then draw, paint, or cut out features. Glue the cutouts in place.

2. To make the holder, cut a rectangle of lightweight cardboard. Place it on the back of the mask and tape the top and the sides of the rectangle, leaving the bottom open.

3. Put the end of a ruler into this "pocket," and you can hold the mask in front of your face.

JEWELRY BOX

(candy box with cardboard lid, lightweight fabric, white glue and water, plastic bowl, lace, string of craft pearls, ribbon)

1. In a small plastic bowl, mix white glue with a little water. Set aside, along with a paintbrush.

2. To cover the box lid, place the fabric right-side down on a flat surface. Place the lid right-side down in the middle of the fabric.

3. Measure a few inches out from the edge of the box lid so the fabric will wrap around the edges to the inside of the lid. Mark the fabric and cut it out.

4. With a paintbrush, spread the glue mixture on the outside of the lid. Press the outside of the lid on top of the fabric. Cut a diagonal line in the fabric to each corner of the lid. Spread glue on the outside and inside edges of the lid. Wrap the fabric up and inside the box lid. Add more glue if necessary. Let dry.

5. If there are sections inside the candy box, cut pieces of fabric and glue them inside the bottom of the box.

6. Decorate the outside lid with lace, pearls, and ribbon.

NEWSPAPER-YARN CREATURE

(newspaper, yarn, felt, paper)

1. Roll newspaper loosely. Bend, twist, and tape the roll into a creature shape.

2. Squeeze glue onto the roll and wrap it with yarn. Fill in small areas with pieces of yarn and glue.

3. Cut features from felt and glue them in place.

PLASTIC-FOAM PUZZLE
(plastic-foam tray, pencil, permanent markers or crayons)

1. Draw a picture on the back of a plastic-foam tray. Use a sharpened pencil to punch tiny holes close together along the lines you have drawn. Push the pieces out.

2. Color both sides of the puzzle pieces, using different colors. You can use either side of the puzzle pieces to make colorful pictures.

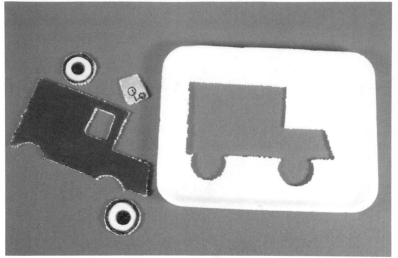

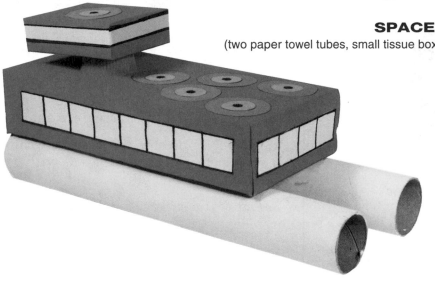

SPACE VEHICLE
(two paper towel tubes, small tissue box, gelatin box, construction paper, plastic lid)

1. Cover two paper towel tubes, a small tissue box, and a gelatin box with construction paper.

2. Glue the tubes to the bottom of the tissue box. Glue a small plastic lid between the tissue box and the gelatin box.

3. Add windows and other decorations made from paper.

WIGGLY CATERPILLAR
(cardboard egg carton, yarn, paper)

1. Cut twelve cups from a cardboard egg carton. Make a small hole in the bottom of each cup.

2. Tie a knot at one end of a long piece of yarn, and string the other end through the holes in the cups. String the cups on the yarn in the same direction.

3. When the twelve cups are strung together, knot the other end.

4. The knot at the first egg cup will be the nose of the caterpillar. Add paper eyes.

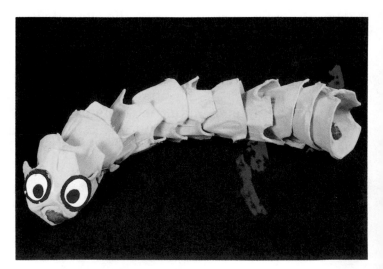

CIRCLES BEAR
(plate, bowl, cup, juice glass, construction paper or poster board)

1. Trace around a plate on construction paper or poster board to make one big circle for the body of the bear. Trace around a bowl to make the head.

2. Trace around a cup for the legs and ears of the bear. Trace around a juice glass for the eyes and a nose.

3. Cut out all the circles and glue them together to make the bear. Draw on a mouth.

NATURE BRACELET
(poster board; dried beans, peas, or barley; yarn)

1. Cut a strip of poster board to fit around your wrist.

2. Glue on dried beans, peas, or barley for decoration.

3. Punch a hole in each end and string a piece of yarn through the holes. Tie the bracelet around your wrist.

RACCOON PUPPET
(cardboard food container, felt, fabric)

1. Wash and dry a cardboard food container like one in which peanuts are packaged.

2. Place the bottom of the container on a piece of felt and trace around the edge with a pencil or marker. Cut out the circle and glue it to the bottom of the container for the top of the puppet.

3. Cut felt ears and glue them to opposite sides of the container. Measure the container and cut a piece of felt to fit all the way around it. Glue the felt in place.

4. Make eyes, a nose, and a mouth from felt. Attach them with glue.

5. Cut a piece of fabric to fit around the inside edge of the container and to cover part of your arm. Spread some glue around the inside edge and wait until glue is tacky.

6. Press the fabric into the glue and let dry. Place your arm and hand inside the container to move your puppet.

MOON ROCKET GAME
(quart-size cardboard milk carton, construction paper, five wooden clothespins, poster board)

1. Wash and dry a quart-size milk carton. Cut off the top. Cover the carton with construction paper.

2. Create a moon scene with stars and a rugged landscape made from cut paper or markers.

3. Use five wooden clothespins for the rockets. For the rocket fins, cut V shapes from poster board and glue them to the inside of the clothespins.

4. Place the "moon" milk carton on the floor in front of you. Hold each rocket by its fin, at waist level. Then drop it, trying to land it in the moon.

5. Take turns with a friend. The first player to score ten landings is the winner.

NATURE PAPERWEIGHT
(clear plastic bottle, heavy cardboard, poster paint, stones, dried flowers, leaves)

1. Wash and dry a clear plastic bottle. Cut about a third of it from the bottom and discard the top.

2. Place the cut end on a piece of heavy cardboard, trace around it, and cut it out, making it slightly larger. Paint it green.

3. Glue small stones, flowers, and leaves on the green cardboard.

4. Glue the bottom half of the plastic bottle on top.

PHOTO HOLDER
(photos, two plastic-foam trays, table knife, plastic wrap, sandpaper, a large needle, yarn)

1. Choose five favorite photos. Cut a circle around each person or animal face in each photo.

2. Cut the sides from two identical plastic-foam trays, creating two pieces the same size.

3. On one piece, draw circles a little smaller than the photos. Press along each circle with a table knife until the circle can be pulled out. Smooth the edges with sandpaper if necessary.

4. Cut and glue a piece of plastic wrap to cover one side of the tray. Spread glue around each circle and place a picture, face down on top of the plastic wrap, covering the circle.

5. Glue the second plastic-foam tray to cover the wrap and the back of the pictures. Place something heavy on top until the glue dries.

6. With a large needle and yarn, sew around the edges, as shown. To make a hanger, thread a piece of yarn through the center of the back and tie a bow.

SCRATCH-A-PICTURE
(white plastic jug, nail, poster paint, rag, poster board)

1. Soak a white plastic jug in warm water to soften it for cutting. Cut a square section from the side of the jug.

2. With a pencil, sketch a picture on the plastic. Go over the sketch with a nail, scratching the picture into the plastic. (The more scratches, the more your design will show.)

3. Spread black poster paint over the picture. Then wipe over it with a dry rag to remove the paint that is not in the nail grooves.

4. Glue the picture to a piece of poster board. Attach a yarn hanger to the back.

BOX-AND-BAG HORSE
(two small boxes, one medium-sized box, two small brown paper bags, construction paper, old newspaper)

1. To make the body of the horse, use one medium-sized box. Use two small boxes for the legs and hooves.

2. Cover the boxes with construction paper. Glue the boxes together.

3. Stuff one small brown paper bag with rolled-up newspaper. Tape it to the body for the neck and head of the horse.

4. Cut a tail and mane from another small brown paper bag. Attach them with glue. Cut circles from the bag for spots and glue them on the horse. Add features with paper and markers.

HAPPY BIRTHDAY POP-UP CARD
(construction paper)

1. Fold an 8 1/2-by-11-inch piece of construction paper in half the long way. Then fold it in half the narrow way.

2. Open the card. At the point where the folds meet, cut and glue balloons, working from the center out and up. Trim with scissors around the balloons.

3. Write "Happy Birthday to you, (add name)" on the balloons. Make a drawing of a clown holding the balloons with his dog. Write another message in the card.

4. Fold the card with the balloon section inside. On the front of the card, glue another piece of paper and write "It's your special day!"

5. When the card is opened, the balloons should pop up.

MAKE-IT-YOURSELF PUZZLE
(large cereal box, masking tape, permanent markers)

1. Cut the front from an empty box of cereal. Put masking tape on all four sides, folding it over the edge.

2. Working on a newspaper, color the tape with permanent markers.

3. Cut the picture into several pieces, like a puzzle. Scramble the pieces and try to put the picture back together again.

LEAFY PAPERWEIGHT
(smooth rock, small leaves, poster paint, clear nail polish)

1. Paint one side of a small leaf with poster paint.

2. While the paint is still wet, press the leaf wet-side down on the rock. Carefully lift up the leaf. Repeat several times to complete the pattern.

3. After the prints have dried, coat the rock with clear nail polish to preserve the design.

MUSIC-PAGE NOTES
(paper, felt, spring-type clothespins)

1. Draw a musical note on a piece of paper to use as a pattern. Cut out the pattern and pin it on a piece of felt.

2. Cut out the felt note. Make another one the same size.

3. Glue one felt note to each of two spring-type clothespins. Use them to hold your page of music in place.

GIRAFFE
(paper towel tube, construction paper)

1. Cover a paper towel tube with glue and yellow construction paper.

2. Cut up from the bottom for the legs and down from the top for the neck and head.

3. Make small cuts down on either side of the horns, and fold forward for the head.

4. Cut spots from brown paper. Cut out eyes, a nose, and hooves from black paper. Glue them in place.

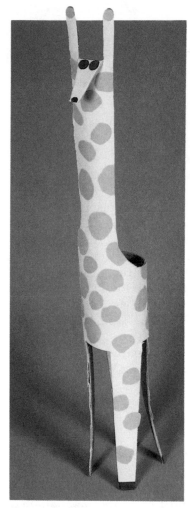

THREAD-SPOOL LIGHTHOUSE
(thread spools, construction paper)

1. Cover spools of different sizes with glue and construction paper. Glue the spools together with the smaller spools on top.

2. Add windows and the door.

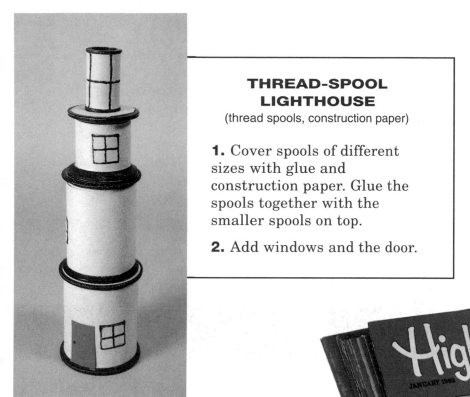

MAGAZINE HOLDER
(heavy cardboard box, old magazines)

1. Find a heavy cardboard box the right size to hold your magazines.

2. Cut it down, making a fancy edge if you wish.

3. Cut pictures from old magazines and glue them all over the outside of the box.

MATERIAL INDEX